Abou

Sarah Harrington is from North London and now lives in Hertfordshire. This is her debut novel.

About the Author

Dear Grace,

Hope you enjoy,
Love
from
Sarah
x x

All the 7s

Sarah Harrington

All the 7s

Vanguard Press

VANGUARD PAPERBACK

© Copyright 2023
Sarah Harrington

The right of Sarah Harrington to be identified as author of
this work has been asserted by her in accordance with the
Copyright, Designs and Patents Act 1988.

All Rights Reserved

No reproduction, copy or transmission of this publication may be
made without written permission. No paragraph of this publication
may be reproduced, copied or transmitted save with the written
permission of the publisher, or in accordance with the provisions
of the Copyright Act 1956 (as amended).

Any person who commits any unauthorised act in relation to this
publication may be liable to criminal prosecution and civil claims
for damages.

A CIP catalogue record for this title is
available from the British Library.

ISBN 978 1 80016 641 7

This is a work of fiction. Names, characters, businesses, places,
events and incidents are either the product of the author's
imagination or used in a fictitious manner. Any resemblance to
actual persons, living or dead, or actual events is purely
coincidental.

Vanguard Press is an imprint of
Pegasus Elliot Mackenzie Publishers Ltd.
www.pegasuspublishers.com

First Published in 2023

Vanguard Press
Sheraton House Castle Park
Cambridge England

Printed & Bound in Great Britain

This book is dedicated to my wonderful family and friends who have supported me in every way and stood by me throughout the years, and to Glen, who helped me get my mojo back. And last but not least, in memory of my beautiful Grandee, who inspired me throughout her fabulous life.

PART ONE
49 YEARS OLD

2019

1

I can sense danger. I find myself standing in a snowstorm, in a car park that I don't recognise and beside me is Layla. We are trying to escape from the blizzard, which is no normal flurry of snow, it is a deluge which is threatening to overwhelm us. Every car in the huge car park is covered in a thick blanket of snow and we are up to our ankles in it. I notice that other people are going about their business, with no sign of fear or alarm. A little boy in a bright red hat and mittens throws a snowball at his dad, who laughs and tries to dodge the missile. A group of teenagers lark about, throwing snowballs at each other, whilst screaming and laughing as they connect. These people are somehow oblivious to the danger that I can sense. Maybe they aren't in any danger? It's only snow after all, isn't it?

I somehow know that Layla can't start her car as the steering wheel has frozen solid. She is wearing a thick woollen bobble hat which looks a bit silly on her, not her usual stylish self. She is also wearing sunglasses and they are so huge that I can see my full reflection in the brown lenses, and I realise I have no clothes on. Oh

God! I panic. Where are my clothes? Layla doesn't seem to notice that I am naked, so maybe other people won't notice. But we're in public!

I dimly realise that I am dreaming, as I start to wrap a bedsheet around me. The sheet has miraculously found its way into my hand, and I realise that the sheet makes my body invisible—great! But people will think I'm a ghost and they will only see my head. I decide that I don't care.

Layla begins to panic, pointing at a raging fire that is blazing its way over towards us and we start to run away from the flames that are fast approaching us, over the top of an Edwardian style building to the right side of the car park.

I don't understand how the snow is not dampening the flames. I have the familiar feeling of dread as we run. We come across an empty car which is not covered in a thick layer of snow, a blue Land Rover. Perfect, I think. As I hurriedly get into the driver's seat, Layla gets into the back seat. Why are you in the back? There's space in the front? I think, and I somehow manage to get the car started despite the interior, but not the exterior, being covered, bizarrely, in thick snow.

I start to reverse the car and the sat-nav begins to give directions, but then I notice that it starts to speak in a conversational way, as if it has conscious thought.

'Zoe, make sure you put your seat belt on and drive like Si,' the sat-nav says.

How does the sat-nav know about Layla's partner Si? I press my foot on the brake and, in a state of panic and fear, I smash the sat-nav apart with a tyre iron that has found its way into my hand. This feels like a set-up.

From nowhere, a woman with long blonde hair gets into the front passenger seat of the car. Layla doesn't react and I say nothing, thinking the woman must want to escape the fire with us. The woman is not someone I have ever seen before, I am sure of that. She is an attractive woman, wearing a white nurse's uniform with short sleeves. On her right arm is a tattoo which looks like Roman numerals: XII XI MMXIX. Wow, I'm dreaming but I seem to know these numbers. I have never been able to decipher these, so how do I know them now? *Remember these numbers, Zoe!* my inner voice says. I will. I will remember them.

As is the way in dreams, the next time I turn to look at the woman sitting next to me, she has morphed into a human-size Buddha with a shiny bronze coating and a smiling serene face. Strangely, I feel calm next to her, despite the fire that is not only raging out of control but seems to be alive, aware and reaching for us, a living entity. The fire wants to destroy me, it feels personal. I manage to keep ahead of the fire, which is following me as I drive, and I look to my right and see that the flames are now not only behind but on the right-hand side of the road, burning up the tarmac. I look to my left and see a turning which leads to a huge hill, surely the fire can't go uphill? Then Layla starts to shout at me from the back seat.

'Don't turn left! Carry straight on!'

Why is she saying that?

I carry on ahead, and the steering wheel starts to pull itself towards the right, intending to take me into the path of the fire. My hands clench tightly on the wheel as I struggle to keep control of the car, my panic rising

I start to wake from my dream, feeling thankful that it was just a dream but wracking my brain to process what it all means. I start to feel woozy and unsure whether I am partially asleep. And then I feel the dread. I briefly struggle to move, but my frozen body and alert mind incapacitate me, so I give up the fight, resigning myself to the visit.

Here we go again. Eyes closed, the familiar radio static in my head, increasing in volume. An ominous feeling, this is bad! Stop it! Don't allow it! But knowing this is inevitable. Then the pressure on the end of the bed—is the night visitor leaning? Sitting? I am too exhausted to fight, waiting for the conclusion.

Suddenly, and for the first time, there is a change. From outside my open bedroom window, I hear the frightening sound of an injured cat's eerie child-like screech, which registers with me and seems to startle the visitor. The weight by my feet eases instantly and the visitor retreats, the doomed feeling disappearing almost instantaneously. He has left my room.

But then, mere seconds later, and for the first time in the visitor's reign, I can hear him advancing on me. What is this? The visitor is walking up the stairs outside my bedroom slowly but with a heavy determined stomp, almost mocking me… as if he is mirroring my thought of, 'Here we go again.'

And again, an interruption. Billy's raised but muffled voice, arguing with someone on the phone, more than likely a girl. The visitor disappears yet again, and I struggle to move. I blink hard a few times to summon the will to get my strength back and pull myself together. I will splash my face with water, I think. I will go downstairs. But I start to drift off again, with a false sense of security. And I then sense him back in the room. My eyes closed, I feel the dread, and then the weight on the end of the bed once again and the bed covers are pulled back from my feet.

Then another change to his usual routine, I feel his weight behind me as I lie curled on my side, in some type of sick representation of "spooning", and, to my horror, yet another first for the visitor, which causes my heart to flutter in panic, he speaks.

"Someone always gets hurt…"

2

I wake up with vivid memories of last night's dreams and then I remember the visit. And so it continues, I think, and I get out of bed with a feeling of tired resignation. Seven years ago was the last time the visitor came to me at night. Can I expect him at age fifty-six? Age sixty-three? When will this end?

During the night, a thick layer of snow has carpeted the garden and, pulling up the wooden slatted blinds and looking through the leaded window which frames the gorgeous scene, I revel in the cosiness and warmth of my home, contrasted with the chill outside.

The sky is no shade of grey, it is as white as the snow. The only other colour I can detect is the dark grey/black of the tree branches glimpsed under the blanket of snow. A grey-and-white vista, so beautiful, so stark.

Nature's simple beauty is especially appreciated the morning following a night visit. The beauty of nature means so much to me, making me feel grateful to be alive and bringing me an element of peace. Tears well in my eyes and I don't know why.

I try to imagine how cold it must be outside but I can't, as the warmth of my bedroom is not allowing my attempts at fantasy.

I make my first coffee of the morning, a delicious latte, enjoying the aroma as much as the taste, and sit at my work desk, watching the snowflakes fall. I reminisce on being a child and letting the snowflakes land in my hand so that I could try to see the intricate patterns, pink fingers stiff and stinging inside warm mittens.

Enjoying the view, my mind continues to drift back to being young, so excited to get outside when the snow arrived, as soon as humanly possible. But now, having reached middle age, the overriding plan of action is now of a practical nature, Have I left anything outside that I shouldn't have? Will the pipes freeze? As the minor concerns fade away as quickly as they arrived, I feel compelled to hibernate and just marvel at the beauty. I like to have background music on while I work, so I think of a song to fit my current mellow but slightly weary mood. I still feel a little self-conscious when I speak to Alexa so bluntly, as it feels so alien, but I'm sure I will get used to it.

'Alexa, play Someone you Loved by Lewis Capaldi.' The mellow sounds come through the speaker and I start to think back about my past relationship with Adam. Did I ever love him? I honestly don't know. But certainly it's the closest I ever got to loving a man.

I'm staying in, I think. I have no idea what day it is, which is no real surprise as it is that confusing period between Christmas and New Year when days of the week don't matter. With no plans on going anywhere and no one needing me now, my plans to write my story now begin.

As long as I can remember, I have always felt that there is way more to understand in the universe, both the physical and the spiritual realms. How do I begin to explain my truth? How not to come across as delusional, naive or, perhaps most worrying of all, mentally unwell? I need to tell my story.

For those that don't believe in monsters.

3

Putting pen to paper feels cathartic. I am exhausted and this needs to end. I will work my way backwards, through the years, back to a confused seven-year-old girl who was afraid of the dark, terrified of nightmares and dark visitors.

Now forty-nine years of age, I am seemingly unlike many other females nearing fifty, in that I am loving the ageing process, despite the inevitable slow but steady physical degeneration that comes with each advancing year. To be more sure of oneself and more content in one's own skin brings a sense of satisfaction and completeness that was completely missing from my teens to my early forties.

I often hear women mourning the loss of the feeling of being desirable to the opposite sex, whereas I find it very empowering. Feeling 'invisible' to the opposite sex brings me a sense of freedom to be myself and please myself. I have enjoyed being a granddaughter, daughter, sister, friend and mother to my loved ones.

Despite learning to love and accept myself and feeling more content as the years advance, something in me has shifted. My subconscious mind has been sending me messages of increasing urgency.

First, to try to decipher my dreams from last night. The frozen pipes in Layla's car and the frozen interior of the Land Rover must just be related to the snow. Snow wasn't forecast, or if it was, I was unaware of it. However, I remember padding around barefoot on the tiled kitchen floor yesterday and thinking it was chilly underfoot.

As usual in my dreams, I am running scared and being hunted. No surprise there. The sat-nav starting to come alive is no surprise to me as this is something I joke about with Layla. We are always telling the inanimate but irritating sat-nav to shut up or to stop being so stupid. The woman with the long blonde hair? She intrigues me but I don't know who she could be. I am always especially fascinated when I dream of somebody whom I know for sure that I have never seen before. I remember the woman had a tattoo on her arm, which I must try to decipher. I seemed to know the number in my dream, but I can't remember it now. I do remember telling myself to remember the number, which frustrates me. The Buddha is clearly a symbol of peace and serenity. Perhaps spiritual awakenings? Is it a lucky sign? I don't know.

For a few years, I have been typing my dreams into a notes app on my phone. Prior to the invention of mobile phones, or more accurately, prior to their popularity, I have been writing dreams in a diary, for as long as I can remember. Today, I write my notes out in full rather than use my phone app. The sound of 'Breaking Me' by Topic plays on the radio, a fitting background to the task at hand.

My dreams have always been what I describe as "epic", in that I am mostly aware that I am asleep but can, often, direct the dreams to suit me in some way. I have learnt that this is called lucid dreaming.

Nearly every dream I have ever had involves being chased by a variety of horrors, including witches, ghosts, aliens and even gorillas, or natural elements of fire, tsunamis and earthquakes. I always manage to escape from whatever horror is chasing me, but the dreams tire me out, and when the visitor comes at night, I know I am not dreaming any more. Is it the visitor I am running from?

A pattern that I have clearly identified as the years go by is that the nights that the visitor comes, elements of my dreams from that night occur in my waking hours one or sometimes two days later. I wonder whether the timeframe is more like a week or more, but I don't connect the dots as the dream isn't as fresh in my mind. These occurrences can be vague or quite specific but I long ago ruled out coincidence. One of the main questions that I ask myself is, does the visitor cause me to see things before they happen or am I more "prophetic" these nights, hence sensing the visitor?

Over the years, I have also identified a physical symptom or reaction to the visits. The day following a visit, and for a few days after, my neck is stiff, and I struggle to turn my head fully to the left. What is the connection? I honestly don't know. But the closest I can guess is that the strain of being pinned down causes stiffness in my neck.

I close my eyes and rub my neck. I can live with the neck aches, but I am exhausted, mentally and physically, and I am desperate for a conclusion. I no longer want to coast along, with a façade of contentment. I feel the need to cleanse myself and have concluded that now is the right time to try to rid myself, finally, of the dark entity that has plagued me every seven years.

All the 7s.

4

I have been seeing a hypnotherapist, Dan, for the last three months. I found Dan online and liked his website. When I arrived at his home for my first appointment, he came to meet me in his front drive, where I had parked.

A tall, trim, good-looking black guy with a disarming smile greeted me. I had imagined a small bespectacled plump man for some reason. I instantly sensed that Dan was a good person, and this was meant to be. Dan lead me to his treatment room, a purpose-built single storey building reached by walking through his back garden.

My first impressions of the treatment room were that it was warm and welcoming, but perhaps a little too bright for hypnotism, with the white blinds permanently open. I was proved wrong on this point, as it turned out that I could be hypnotised very easily, despite the daylight shining in. A huge, battered leather sofa became my treatment couch for ninety minutes nearly every week.

I initially went to see Dan for smoking cessation and weight management hypnotherapy. The combination of the messages sent to my subconscious and the hours of talking issues through with Dan resulted in me giving up smoking and leaving my bad binge eating habits in the past. I had smoked since I was fourteen years of age and had never managed to go even a few days without a cigarette or ten, twenty on a night out.

I feel so proud that I have broken this nasty habit, although I do still dream regularly that I smoke, which is perhaps understandable, as this was a 35-year habit. My binge eating had started when I was a teenager and Dan has given me coping mechanisms to use in my daily life that, combined with the messages sent to my subconscious, are working so far.

During our sessions, perhaps inevitably, I started to touch on my dreams and, a month ago, I started to tentatively mention my visitor.

I played it down and even began to talk myself out of it at one point, but Dan was adamant that we needed to look into the visits further.

At my second from last session, following a long discussion and a fair amount of backtracking on my part, I agreed to go under to enable Dan to try to get answers from my subconscious to try to discover the cause of my visits. The idea was to go back from my current age right back to birth, to find out whether I had experienced any trauma.

The hypnotism technique always involved Dan making me believe that one hand felt like it was holding a bucket being filled with water, resulting in my hand feeling heavy and dropping into my lap. Then, I was made to think that the other hand was holding a bunch of helium balloons, causing my hand to raise higher and higher. Then, both hands were relaxed on to my lap with a pre-defined auto suggestion, namely Dan patting his finger lightly on my hands. I would then answer Dan's scripted questions in the affirmative by raising my forefinger and keep my fingers on my lap if my reply was negative.

I had always gone under very easily, but this session was different. My subconscious wasn't playing ball, at all.

Dan's soothing hypnotising technique sent me under initially and, as always, I felt a sense of calm and a dream-like sensation as I was taken deeper. Although the full bucket and helium balloons trick worked for me, two words kept flashing up behind my closed eyes in thick white capital letters: *Go Away*. It distracted me and focussed all my attention, preventing me from listening to Dan's questions.

When Dan brought me out of my hypnotised state, he seemed disappointed that he couldn't help me on this occasion. Or, more accurately, disappointed that I was blocking him from helping me. When our session had finished, I drove home that afternoon and slept for over three hours. The internal battle had left me exhausted.

The following week, after a few back-and-forth phone calls, I agreed to try again, but the same thing happened, and as I left Dan's treatment room, I knew I wouldn't be returning. A wave of sadness came over me on the drive home, as I thought of Dan and all the help he had given me. I had become quite attached to him and enjoyed our sessions.

When I got home, I was shattered, and prior to going for a sleep, I called Layla and updated her on the outcome of the session, or lack of.

'Do you feel like he's stopping you?' asked Layla, referring to the visitor.

'I just don't know. It could be my own subconscious mind is not allowing the intrusion.'

Back to the drawing board for me, then.

5

Layla called me this morning and asked me to meet up, and though I felt reluctant to leave the warmth of my home, we meet in the park, the air bitingly cold but refreshing, a welcome change from the heated closeted home I have been spending way too much time in lately. The snow has begun to melt, leaving the usually pristine grass and trees strangely shabby, reminding me of a half-melted gritty snowman. We were wrapped up warm and sipping our takeaway coffees along the way. Layla, a friend from my teenage years, has always shared a certain spirituality with me and always has a comical turn of phrase.

'Maybe it's a ghost!' she beams. I had mentioned to her that my visitor was back and morphing into a talking, not to mention "spooning", creature. A passer-by decked out in an overkill of winter layers, glances at her briefly, flashing a quick smirk. I wait until we are clear of the man. His child-like bobble hat gives me a flashback to my own dream featuring Layla in a silly looking woollen bobble hat.

'Possibly, but I need to find out. It's like, what if it ramps up even more and materialises?' I half laugh and she joins in.

'Whoooh!' Layla shakes a gloved hand in the air, and we laugh.

'What about an exorcism?' asks Layla, and she notices my dubious frown. 'Or, I know, a clairvoyant! I've seen this woman, Dana, before and she's spot on. We could go together.'

'Ooh, I'd be up for that, definitely. When can we go and see her?'

'I'll call her and book us both in. You can go first, you need to get this sorted.' Layla pauses.

'Hopefully.' She smiles.

'I need to try something, I'm just so exhausted in the daytime after the struggles in the night.'

'I'm jealous,' says Layla. 'I could do with a nocturnal lover.' She bumps my arm in jest.

'It's not good, Layla!' I pull a joke grumpy face and she squeezes my arm.

'I know,' she says, and we continue to walk along together, changing the subject to our respective work lives, our adult children's lives, the UK's impending withdrawal from the EU and, most interesting of all, gossip and intrigue, as we always do when we are together. We laugh about a male friend of ours from our school days who had accidentally posted a live video of himself on Facebook. He had been lying in bed, making some strange noises, including groans and, most amusing of all, a kind of snuffling noise. Only the top half of his head was visible in the video, which was a sweet relief. And we discuss how we are both thankful that we didn't have the internet around when we were young.

'I dread to think what type of things we would have posted,' says Layla.

'Oh, don't. And the amount of boys we would have stalked.'

As always when spending time with Layla, I came away from our time together feeling more relaxed and my problems feel manageable somehow.

6

Excited that the day of the visit to the clairvoyant has finally arrived, I drive to meet Layla at the address she gave me over the phone. The drive has been a predictable pain, the sat-nav taking me well out of my way as usual. *Maybe the stupid sat-nav is possessed,* I think. This thought brings back vague notions of a sat-nav issue in a dream. Was that last night, I wonder?

I pull up at the destination, waving to Layla who is standing by her car, talking on the phone. I unplug the sat-nav and throw it on to the passenger seat. At least I know which general direction to head in on the way home. The houses in the cul-de-sac are modern but large and showy, lots of huge windows and roomy drives with expensive cars parked outside. This lady must be genuine, I think, but realise instantly that this is a naïve assumption, as I have no idea of her circumstances.

I air kiss Layla as she finishes her call and we then agree on some pointers prior to knocking on the front door.

'She only knows my first name, doesn't she?'

'Not even your name; I just said I was bringing a friend,' explains Layla.

This is perfect, as I have my doubts about clairvoyants, and I want the woman to know as little as possible about me. She doesn't live near to us, which is one good point, and she couldn't possibly search online for me without my name.

'Right,' I say. 'I have no wedding ring, and no tan line where the ring should be, so she will know I'm not married. I just wonder how much she can pick up from me by just looking.'

'She's genuine, I promise! You'll see.' Layla has seen the clairvoyant before, and I trust her judgement but just want to cover all the bases.

We walk to the front door and ring the bell. Layla had already told me that Dana is an attractive curvaceous woman of about our age with long blonde hair. When she opens the door, I can instantly feel a nice aura about her, so first impressions are good. I briefly remember a clairvoyant that I had once seen years ago who was incredibly stressed looking and greeted me at the front door in an almost irritated fashion, so I am relieved.

'Hello ladies,' says Dana. 'Come through.'

She leads us through a wide, light hallway into the open-plan kitchen. *Wow,* I think, *gorgeous place.* There is a large kitchen island to the left, surrounded by modern glossy kitchen units and a gorgeous light filled conservatory to the right, with a huge bronze Buddha sitting serenely on a sideboard. *Ah,* I think, *there's the*

Buddha from last night's dream. I'm not even remotely surprised any more.

'Would you like a glass of water?' Dana asks, and we both accept. As we sip our drinks, Layla chats with Dana briefly while I soak up the gorgeous décor.

'So, who is going first?' she asks. I raise my hand and Layla says, 'My friend,' gesturing to me. I smile, as Layla has remembered to stick to our plan of not giving my name.

Dana leads me to her treatment room. Wow, this is finally happening, I think. Although the wait between discussing the potential visit with Layla and now has only been a few days, it has filled my thoughts constantly.

Dana extends her hand to the direction of a pale blue chair that looks extremely comfortable and inviting. 'Please, take a seat.'

I sit down and exhale gently. The chair doesn't disappoint.

'Do you practise clairvoyancy?' Dana begins by asking.

'Ah, no I don't.'

Dana seems surprised. 'Well, you could.'

'I know what you mean, I think I'm, I don't know, quite… spiritual?' Almost embarrassed to admit it.

'I could see it straight away. You could do what I do. Why don't you?'

I'm scared, I think. 'I would be too eager to please, I think, and I would want to tell people what they want to hear, and probably make things up.' I smile. 'So I steer clear of it. I'm happy with someone else doing it.' Dana smiles but I can sense that she thinks this is a wasted gift.

'Okay, so how can I help you today?' Dana asks and I get a definite sense of a very calm and kind individual, the warmth seeming to emanate across the room. I feel that this lady can help me. I feel so calm and sleepy, perhaps a mixture of the lighting and calm energy, with no outside distractions. Has my water been drugged? *Stop it, stop being paranoid,* I think, and try to relax.

The artfully designed healing room, decorated in muted creams and taupes is dimly lit due to a thick cream vertical slatted blind almost cutting out natural light but it feels warm and inviting, almost hazy. I can smell a gorgeous aroma, possibly jasmine, and see a scented candle burning on a glass side table.

Dana's gentle, positive energy eases me in to building up the courage to risk the potential embarrassment of laying my cards on the table. We begin by talking of general day-to-day matters and she then opens and explains to me her own spiritual experience, placing me further at ease.

As she speaks, as often happens with me, I don't realise straight away, but vestiges of my dream return and Dana is the woman that was in the car with me; there is no doubt in my mind about that. The nurse's uniform I would think denotes a caregiver, or someone giving you treatment. This was meant to be I think, and this thought both comforts and encourages me. I then think of my three angels dream from years ago, a dream that I think of periodically and try to decipher. Was Dana one of the angels?

Dana continues. 'When I was a child, I could sense that I was different, I could feel spirits around me. But my parents discouraged my spiritual side, and I was made to feel ashamed.'

'Ah, I'm sorry to hear that,' I say.

I decide now is the time. With no preamble, I blurt out, 'I have a dark visitor and I would like him to let me go.'

She doesn't widen her eyes, doesn't pause, but she "sees". 'Ah,' she says, looking over my left shoulder, 'he's hiding. He likes to hide. You picked him up when you were a little girl; does that make sense to you?'

'Yes,' I reply, my voice cracking.

Dana begins to chant a healing spell in a soft voice tinged with urgency, and continues repeating the words, repeatedly. I catch Dana saying, 'Go in peace,' and inexplicably think of *The Exorcist* and my mind wanders further as she continues.

I wonder whether chanting will help; they are just words, surely? This visitor has been with me for nearly half a century. And then I begin to question myself as to why I have waited this long to get help. Do I want the visitor to stay? But, as Dana continues, I make a concerted effort to relax myself enough to absorb her calming intonations and try to stay clear of negative thoughts in order to try to help her efforts.

'Do you feel okay?' she asks when the healing spell has presumably been chanted enough to make a change. I smile.

'Yes, I'm fine,' I reply, although I do feel light-headed but calm. Dana then promises to email over the healing spell for me to use if I need a "boost" and I joke with her that I may miss the visitor if he really has gone, but I am only half-joking. He is like a part of me, I think, as familiar as a member of my family, as he has been with me for so long. I thank her sincerely for her help and go to call Layla through for her session.

Back in the conservatory area, I approach the huge Buddha statue, stroking it softly, and I whisper, 'Thank you.' I then feel immediately silly and glance around to check that no one has entered the open-plan room and overheard me.

Slowly looking around the large airy room, taking everything in, I begin to feel faint, and my legs feel shaky yet kind of hollow. I slowly move towards the leather sofa by the window, steadying myself by holding on to tables and chair backs as I work my way over, determined not to collapse on the floor. When I reach the sofa, I fall slightly sideways on to the arm in a half faint, but thankfully I manage to stay conscious. Gasping for air, in through the nose, out through the mouth, as I get my breath—is it that way round? I can never remember. I feel generally lighter, as if a heavy weight has been lifted. I scrabble within my mind to find him within me: *where are you? Are you really gone?* I don't understand how that was so easy. I tell myself to be happy, this is how other people feel, unfettered and free but the emptiness is quite stark. It will take some time getting used to, I think, and will become my new norm.

The lightheaded sensation has now nearly passed. I take my phone out of my bag and decide to start sorting through my photos to kill time waiting for Layla to emerge. Flicking my finger to the left through thousands of photos stored on my iPhone, I stop at a photo of Adam and me, taken by who knows whom, probably when I was around mid- to late thirties, standing in a courtyard in Spain, outside a restaurant. I am looking at Adam with a quizzical look and he has his well-worn "naughty" smirk on, the one where he has just said something inappropriate. But what catches my eye is the dark shadow over my left shoulder. The sun is blazing in the photo and the only natural shadow being cast is Adam's across the right side of my body where we are leaning slightly into one another, to appear close. If not in our hearts, in our stance.

The shadow looks out of place. I zoom in by pinching and releasing my fingers and the shadow is vaguely distinguishable as a face. What the hell? I reduce the photo back to its normal size and flick through more photos at speed until I come across a photo of me on a sofa at a party, aged around fourteen,

36

with a friend on either side leaning in towards me, a female to the left and a male to the right. I am smiling sheepishly in the photo, but my right hand is raised to the photographer as if to say, 'No, don't take this!' as I have a bottle in my left hand that presumably I had been swigging from, given the lack of a glass present. And there, again, is a dark shadow over my left shoulder. This shadow is more blurry when I zoom in, as the photo is older. Also, the photo was not taken on my phone camera, rather it is a photo of a photo. I continue to flick through with an increasing sense of alarm. *How did I never notice this?* I think. *Because you weren't looking for it,* my internal voice replies. Photo after photo of shadows.

When Layla emerges from the treatment room, looking tired but happy, we say our goodbyes to Dana and stroll back to where our cars are parked.

'Shall we get a coffee, somewhere local?' asks Layla. 'We can have a proper catch up and compare notes.'

'Ah, perfect,' I say. 'You know the area better than me, I'll follow you.' I am relieved that I won't have to drive the long distance home just yet, as I need to gather my thoughts and rid myself of the slight headache that is starting to invade my forehead. I decide not to tell Layla about the shadows in the photos, it is just too much. If the visitor has indeed gone for good, it doesn't matter now.

I follow Layla through the unfamiliar streets in my car, excited to tell her how my session had gone and to find out about her own. I realise that my neck ache has completely disappeared, and I smile to myself. Tears of relief roll from my eyes, for everything.

I find a space directly next to Layla in a supermarket car park. We skirt around the side of the shop and walk into the welcoming entrance of an independent little café in the small, smart-looking town centre. After ordering our coffees, we sit in cosy corner seats away from too much foot traffic. The décor is very trendy, all industrial style light fittings, scaffold board tables and huge ornate mirrors, no doubt to give the illusion of space to this tiny seating area. Coupled with the gorgeous aroma of freshly brewed coffee, I feel content.

As we sip our creamy coffees from huge cups, Layla asks, 'So, how did it go?'

I keep it brief and explain to Layla that Dana had chanted a healing spell to get rid of the visitor. I also tell her that my neck ache has completely disappeared.

'Well, you've got him off of your shoulder.' This makes perfect sense, in the twisted reality that I have always lived. As she tells me about her own healing, I think how pleased I am to have Layla to go through this experience with me. This interlude was much needed after the exhausting emotional rollercoaster at Dana's.

Layla notices a few rain spatters on the steamy front window, so we decide to get going in case the weather worsens. When the bill arrives, we joke around as we squabble about who should pay the bill, as we always do, but I win as I remind Layla that she had paid last time.

Glancing at the bill, I notice that the date is 11th December, and yet again this nags at me. Why does that date resonate with me? Have I forgotten someone's birthday? As we make our way out of the cosy seating area to the front of the shop, I glance up at a huge antique style clock on the wall, the hours printed in Roman numerals. Yet another sense of déjà vu, from my dream?

Layla's voice jolts me out of my thought pattern. 'Ooh, it's getting late, we'd better get straight off as it's going to get dark soon.' Layla struggles to see properly when driving in the dark so we tend to keep our meetups to earlier in the day if we plan to drive anywhere. So, rather than check out the local shops, we head straight back to our respective cars. On the way to the car park, Layla asks if I'm okay.

'Yeah, I'm fine. Relieved, really. But I'm not looking forward to this drive.'

'Just follow me and I'll point out the left turning that you need to go down, and I'll then carry straight on to mine.'

'If we can see,' I say, as the rain continues to fall slowly but ominously, in those huge slow drops that indicate worse to come.

As we reach the car park, my eye is drawn to a building to the right of the car park, tall and Edwardian looking, and there's that sense of déjà vu again.

'Shame we brought two cars,' I say, thinking that I would much prefer Layla to be with me in my car.

'Ah, we'll be fine, just go slow. Drive like you're Si,' Layla smiles. My dream again, something about a car and Si. I smile at our shared joke, which refers to Si's partner's driving style, which can only be described as cautious and dangerously slow.

I kiss Layla on the cheek and get into my car, feeling anxious.

7

The rain is coming down hard now. *Oh God,* I think, as I don't know the area and I don't like driving in rain when I don't know where I'm going. After setting the sat-nav, I wait for Layla to pull out, and I wait for other cars to pass so that I can get behind her.

Following Layla, my emotions overwhelm me, and a seemingly endless flood of tears trickles down my face, tears of relief and tears of freedom. I feel that both a mental and a physical weight have been lifted from my shoulders and my search for answers can now be put to bed. I feel free but strangely empty. Can't you just be relieved? I chastise myself.

When we approach the turning that I think I need to turn down, I start to indicate. My heart jumps as I see Layla gesticulating. It doesn't look like she is pointing left and waving goodbye, it looks very much like she is pointing left and shaking her hand back and forth as if to warn me not to go that way.

'Oh, sod it,' I say out loud, and I take the turning. Layla continues on her way in the other direction. If I had followed Layla further, I would have ended miles out of my way, so I'm glad I took the turn. Her hand movements unnerved me, but that's to be expected as I am on edge.

The winding road is long and narrow, and I tense up each time cars fly past too quickly on the other side of the road. I finally reach a roundabout and get on the slip road to head towards home.

The motorway is busy at this time of day. We hadn't considered after work traffic when planning this journey. If we had left Dana's house straight away, we could have missed this, but I don't regret our catch-up, as Layla is the one person I needed to confide in.

Steamed up windows, windscreen wipers at their fastest setting, bright car headlights every which way. Oops, I quickly turn on my own lights. Unaware of how fast I am driving, I suddenly realise that I am flying along the fast lane at 80 miles per hour, way above the speed limit. Pushing my foot gently on the brake, mindful of the cars behind, I slow myself down as much as the traffic will allow.

Gradually settling back in for a sensible drive the rest of the way home, I decide to change the channel on the radio, which is blasting out the melancholy tones of Lewis Capaldi, singing 'Before you Go'. I land on a channel with a strong signal, playing my favourite song, 'Location' by Dave and Burna Boy. I love this song, the beat, the singers' voices. I don't know most of the words, but I don't let that stop me singing along.

Singing loud and feeling good, suddenly, I feel a strong pressure on both of my hands, unnaturally strong, forcing me to turn the steering wheel to the left, pushing me towards the inside lane... the pressure building, as if an unseen force is steering me directly into a car with intent. I instantly think of the visitor—he has only ever prevented me from moving, not actually taken over the control of my body. But I know that it is him.

My heart starts to thud, I cry out 'No! ... Why!' I wail loudly, panic-stricken. He won't leave me. Like an insanely jealous lover, he has decided my fate. With immense effort I fight, but then I am beaten by the pressure and swerve to my left, heart hammering, and, by a split-second margin, I just miss a family packed into an SUV. I hear car horns beeping loudly and from several directions. And the sound of my beating heart loud in my ears.

As I raise a trembling hand to apologise to the panicking family, mouthing 'sorry' as if that is enough of an explanation, the force dissipates. For some inexplicable reason, I remember the nurse/Buddha sitting in the passenger seat and the Roman numerals tattoo on her arm. For some reason, the numerals are important; I hadn't got round to finding out what number they represented. I must do that once I get home. Still shaken up, I try to focus on the road ahead and getting home safely.

I think of—

Suddenly, and without warning, the unnatural force on my hands re-emerges. This time, the unseen force is pulling me to the right, back into the lane of fast-moving traffic. Everything is moving way too fast, time itself seems to have sped up. 11th December! From the clipboard! The nurse from my dream got me to sign! *Stop!* I scream internally and clench my jaw so tight that I feel something inside my mouth click ominously.

The pressure is too much; I fight mentally and physically to no avail. He is stronger than me; he is beating me… please no, please no, stop and, with horror in my heart, I start to see him materialise, first smoky grey and then a thicker less opaque murky grey, and his features start to become clearer. The smile, oh God the evil smile… *I know you so well,* I think, and, for only the second time in my life, he speaks: 'I told you someone always gets hurt.'

I swerve into the fast lane and my fate.

2018
2017
2016
2015
2014
2013

PART TWO
42 YEARS OLD

2012 – 7 years ago
1

I find myself in Dane Avenue, near to where I grew up. Here again? Why do I dream of this place so often? It is daytime and I am walking up the road, past the petrol station. I then go under the bridge that I fear so much. The bridge is dark and cold, always wet even in the summer months, giving off a pulsating feeling of dread. I notice the dark grey, almost black brick walls are covered in graffiti, but it is written in roman numerals. I can't remember how to read numerals. Who does that kind of graffiti? It feels wrong. *Hurry up,* I think, *get to the other side.*

I then spot a lone supermarket trolley rolling steadily towards me and I dodge to the side. With not a person in sight, where did this come from?

I emerge into the bright daylight on the other side of the bridge with a sense of relief. I approach the bus stop and a slim black man with a beard steps out of the bus shelter and stands in front of me. He is standing on the pavement, directly facing me as I walk towards him. Although he has no wings, I know that he is an angel in human form. A feeling of serenity and goodness emanates from him and he reaches up his hand and touches the side of my mouth with his index finger. He then tells me that he will see me again and he will heal "these", which I understand to mean lines either side of my mouth. Have I got lines? I will have to check this out when I am awake.

I walk away from the angel and carry on walking in the direction of my childhood home. Up ahead, coming round the corner of Daneland, to the left, I see Si, Layla's partner.

'Hey,' I call out and Si spots me.

Bizarrely, he starts to back up, with a scared look on his face. I freeze as I think that maybe he can see someone frightening behind me. I slowly look round, and there is no one and indeed nothing behind me. Relieved, my heart fluttering, I look back at Si and he is disappearing backwards round the corner, out of sight. What's wrong with him? I carry on walking and wonder whether, when I turn the corner, I will see Si walking backwards up the entire length of the road.

However, before I reach the corner, up ahead I see an attractive middle-aged blonde lady wearing a white nurse's uniform, and I realise that she is also an angel. She generates the same warmth as the man I have just encountered but edged with more of a sense of authority. She is about two metres in front of me and, as the first angel did, she stops and faces me directly. She is well groomed and glamorous looking, with piercing blue eyes.

The blonde lady says, 'I was going to make you better, but I will leave it for now.' I understand that 'making me better' probably involves me dying. That can wait, I think.

I now find myself outside the postal sorting office. On the opposite side of the road, where the 1970s style flats are usually situated, there is now some type of medical facility. I cross over the road and approach the front entrance via a path. The double doors swing wide open, outwards, and under the bright functional strip lights in the foyer stands a nurse holding a clipboard and pen, with paperwork for me to sign. I walk towards her and then stand to her side to see what I am signing, and I see that there is a date on the paper: 11th December 2019. I sign the paper without question, not bothering to read further. Then I find myself back on the pavement.

I carry on walking up the road and I see a third angel, a short Indian lady wearing doctors' whites and glasses. She doesn't speak but just smiles and points behind me on to the pavement at some bags that I have left behind and she then guides me on to the bus that has pulled up beside me. I realise that I am going on a journey.

Wow, that was something else! I absolutely love this dream, I must try to remember the details. I am so keen to get up straight away and start to note everything down so that I remember. Unfortunately, my mind is keener than my body, as I am too tired to move. This is going straight into my notes app first thing in the morning. ...

As I begin to try to make sense of the dream, the radio static starts in my head and I fight it, as best I can. It works temporarily, quietens, and I start to fall back to sleep. Then I start to become more alert and here comes the static again... I should have known. The amazing dream will inevitably be accompanied by darkness, the feeling of dread. My heart starts to hammer. Knock, knock, let me out.

Calm down, try to wake up fully! Then the pressure on the end of the bed, the covers pulled back from my feet. I hear Billy cough, in the next room, and the pressure disappears. This is proof! He is scared! I think of a furtive rat, scurrying to hide from the presence of humans. Then, after what seems like only a few minutes, the pressure returns. I try to send a mental message to Billy: *Cough again!* As ever, in this state, I can't talk, can't move, that familiar old oppression. When are you going to leave me alone?

With my arms now pinned back above my head, and as I feel the familiar dead weight on my wrists, I don't know what comes over me, but for the first time ever I slowly start to pull my right wrist free. I pull and twist down very slowly, as if I think he won't notice me trying to break free, but it is more than that. I want to see if I can feel a hand, fingers. And as my fingers pull through the "clamp", I distinctly feel the actual shape of his hand, his fingers.

This is too much.

2

The alarm clock goes off and I wake up more tired than when I went to bed last night. As I try to raise myself out of bed, the pain in my neck stops me in my tracks, and I lie back down, feeling defeated.

The visits have ramped up recently. I wonder whether my emotional state encourages the visitor. There certainly seems to be a pattern. But I cannot ignore the ongoing connection with 7. Could this be a self-fulfilling prophecy? Have I somehow manifested the visits subconsciously? I doubt that this will ever be solved, it will just remain a part of my life that I must learn to live with. But I worry that the visits are starting to morph in an alarming way.

I think of the loud crackling radio static sound which accompanies the black-and-white flashes behind my closed eyelids. I can never decipher whether the flashes are physical manifestations of the crackling sound in my ears, but I know that they always come before a visit. My body and mind drift into the situation, which amazes me as I know what is going to happen, and I don't believe that I am completely powerless to stop this, so why not wake myself fully, sit up, turn on a light? Because I feel drugged. I imagine Rohypnol would make me feel this way. This takes me back to many years ago when I decided to force my eyes open and I didn't like what I saw, vowing never to do this again.

Aside from the physical weakness, if I were to guess as to my motives for not fighting harder, and allowing this to happen, I would put it down to a feeling that I don't want to upset the visitor in case the experience worsens somehow. How deranged this seems, almost akin to making a burglar welcome and offering a cup of coffee.

Once I have gathered the will to get up and get on with my day, I grit my teeth and push against the pain in my neck. It is early morning, but light outside, as I sit down with a coffee at the kitchen table, relieved to be awake and feeling better than when I woke up. I think back to the days when the children were small and getting up earlier than them was one of life's little luxuries. I used to sip on a coffee, which tasted even more delicious as I could drink it in peace.

I fire up my iPad and prop it up against a vase of flowers. Opening my notes app, I start to note my dream down while it is fresh in my mind and attempt the decode the particulars. The medical facility being located where it was in my dream makes no real sense to me, as I have always known the building to be residential flats. The bridge is no surprise, as I have had nightmares about this bridge for as long as I can remember. The journey to my childhood home must have some significance as this is also a recurring dream. And it stands to reason that I dream of my childhood home as these were my formative years.

And as for the angels, I feel honoured, as I believe, in my heart of hearts, that three angels came to visit me in my dream state. I think of the man indicating my facial lines and as I do, I subconsciously touch the side of my mouth. As for the second angel, that part of the dream is blatant and not something I want to delve in to too much. Is she somehow the person that will take me away or decide my fate? She seemed so kind, so whatever her involvement in my life, it must be in the form of trying to help me.

The bags that the third angel pointed to would seem to indicate some type of journey that I am going on.

And what to make of the date that I signed up to? 11th December 2019. Working out I will be forty-nine then, my mind then switches to thoughts of the lines on the side of my mouth that were mentioned by the first angel. How vain to focus in on that one point. But I go to the mirror anyway.

At least it is something I can attempt to solve.

3

My relationship with Adam ended in 2005, albeit temporarily as it turned out. It was harder on Adam initially, as I was taking the children with me, and had them to focus my attentions on. But I made it as easy as possible for him to see them and he never failed to spend time with them when he said he would.

Initially, directly after we split, I moved my household contents into storage and moved with the children back to Mum and Dad's for around six weeks. This was a bittersweet time. Going back to my childhood home made me feel like a carefree child again for a short period of time, but I missed my own space, as did my parents.

I managed to find unfurnished rented accommodation five minutes away from Adam, who had stayed at the family home. There was never any question of me staying at the family home and him leaving, for a variety of reasons. We had never married, so I had no legal rights that I was aware of. And at that time, I just wanted to be free of Adam but also free of the house itself where I had been unhappy. And I just didn't want that fight.

We moved close to Adam as opposed to staying in my home town because I had grown to love the area and, crucially, I wanted Adam to have easy accessibility to the children, as I felt that our failed relationship shouldn't have to inconvenience them any more than was necessary.

When we first moved in to the three-bedroom semi, Adam was coming over more and more to help with DIY and odd jobs around the house. Then, one day, we inevitably started a romantic relationship again, sparked by passion, but probably more out of ease than anything else.

I remember well the night it started. Adam had turned up unannounced on my birthday and had presented me with a brand new iPhone. My Nokia had given up the week before and I didn't have the spare cash to shell out on a half-decent phone. I had been adamant that I didn't want to get involved with the whole Apple tie-in, but the phone became my favourite brand. And I was touched that he had been so considerate as he wasn't previously known for being thoughtful with gifts.

Aside from brief visits from well-wishers and receiving some nice gifts throughout the day, it hadn't been a traditional birthday as I was busy decorating the front room in time for a family get-together that I was due to host the following week. Adam mucked in and picked up the traditional takeaway fish and chips for lunch, a meal that we always had when decorating. We spent hours listening to music and chatting whilst painting the walls and ceilings, over the course of two days. I really enjoyed our time together, and I know he did too.

Increasingly over the weekend, there was a weird sexual heat between us that I have never experienced before, and we could both feel it. On the Sunday night, when Billy had gone out for the evening, the sexual tension between us became too much and covered in paint splatters, we rekindled our passion.

Afterwards, we lay on the mattress on my bedroom floor, and I stroked his chest and enjoyed the moment, feeling secure and content lying next to him. It felt exciting, probably because it was our secret and it felt a little naughty. We established, there and then, that this would be happening whenever we could make it happen.

Adam left early in the evening in case Billy came back and caught us together. When he had gone, I played some of my music on iTunes while I lay on the mattress. The uplifting sound of Pitbull's 'Give Me Everything' fitted my mood perfectly and I fell asleep with my new phone on the pillow next to my bed.

I blindly told myself that the situation was fine and suited us both. This carried on until recently. It felt so easy to fall back into that pattern.

Adam was on his best behaviour, as was I, when we rekindled our physical relationship. But inevitably, the facades crumbled. Over time, Adam's drinking increased, and my tolerance decreased. I'm sure that we managed to keep the physical side of our relationship a secret from Darcy and Billy, so as not to complicate things, and they never asked.

About a year ago, Billy was away with goodness knows who, as he keeps his girlfriends separate from us. I think that he is worried that we could get their names wrong and embarrass him. Adam and I took the opportunity to have a romantic night away in a secluded country hotel that I had found on Booking.com. The plan was to book into the hotel, to go clothes shopping in the nearest town and then later go out for a meal and drinks.

It was a gorgeous afternoon when we set off in Adam's car, warm with a light breeze. After a brief argument when I didn't read the Google map on my phone to his satisfaction, and we ended up miles out of the way, we finally arrived at the beautiful, grand hotel. As we got out of the car and crunched over the shingle driveway leading to the entrance, we saw that a magical wedding was taking place on the huge lawn to the side of the hotel, complete with Scottish pipers kitted out in the full garb.

Once checked in, we were shown to our room by a staff member. The ground floor room was spacious and beautifully decorated, with a huge four-poster bed and doors opposite the bed opening to a terrace with stone steps leading down to the grounds. When booking, I had chosen a room that had a balcony or terrace so that we could recreate one of our favourite holiday pastimes, enjoying the outside space in the evening so that we could both smoke and Adam could enjoy a drink. Although not a balcony, to me, the terrace was unique and special.

This place felt perfect, so I was surprised to see that Adam wasn't happy. He was sulking and on edge. I joined him out on the terrace.

'What's wrong?' I asked.

Adam sighed. 'It's too far from anywhere.' He hadn't finished. 'And I don't really want to stay here while there's a wedding party here. Also, we'll have to get cabs to and from the local town centre, and we were supposed to be clothes shopping.'

'We still can!' I suggested, but he was not giving in.

'No, Zoe, I'm not carrying shopping bags while we're out drinking tonight.' Adam knew that his night of drinking would be cut short if we were laden with bags.

I was aghast. In my opinion, we couldn't be in a nicer place.

'Come on, it's lovely here. We can leave the clothes shopping for another day and just get ready and go straight out?'

But he wouldn't snap out of it. After a bit of toing and froing, I asked 'Do you want to leave?'

'Yeah.'

I was so disappointed as I thought this place was so romantic. But with Adam in this kind of mood, staying wouldn't be enjoyable.

So off we went to the reception desk and I complained to a staff member about the room. When offered another, I was forced to say that I wasn't happy in general and wanted a refund. I felt embarrassed that the guy thought the place wasn't up to our standards when, in fact, I thought it exceeded our standards. And I was sad that Adam was reverting to his old self. The truth of the matter was, his drinking was more important than my feelings, and the location got in the way of his drinking plans.

I tried to cheer him up and we went looking for a last-minute hotel room in a town centre location. We drove around for at least an hour, and by this time clothes shops were closing for the day. We pulled over at a train station forecourt and I tried Booking.com on my app, but it wasn't proving helpful, as everywhere local to where we were was booked up for the night. I resorted to asking a cab driver who was parked at the station entrance if he knew of any local hotels that could potentially have any last-minute vacancies.

We eventually arrived at a Holiday Inn, which resembled a depressing grey prison block. The only room available had twin beds and was so spartan that it really did feel like we were in prison. But Adam loved it.

Trying to shake off my disappointment and go with the flow, I had a shower and got ready for our night out. The evening was balmy, and the locals were out in droves. We found a nice pub by the river and sat on tall stools by a high wooden circular table outside.

I tried to push the earlier disappointment from my mind, but the more drunk that Adam got, the more irritated I became. At one point, I wanted to find a nice restaurant, but Adam wasn't keen, as it would interrupt his drinking time, so we stayed in the pub. There was food being served but Adam said, 'You have something. I'm bloated.' I didn't have the confidence to order a plate of food just for myself, so dinner was off for the evening.

The sounds of 'Don't Stop Believin'' by the *Glee* cast came on the sound system outside the pub. We both liked the original by Journey, as the song was played in, and therefore reminded us of, the last scenes of *The Sopranos*, our favourite ever box set. Although the *Glee* version wasn't as good as the original, I still enjoyed hearing it, as I like the song. Somehow, this turned in to an argument that lead to name calling and spite on both sides.

We managed to pull it back a bit, and when we arrived back at the hotel, Adam was in high spirits, but I felt deflated. This had to be the least romantic getaway in the history of the world. The ensuing explosive argument ended with me saying that our clandestine relationship had been fun but couldn't continue if Adam didn't give up drinking.

Adam cried, which tugged on my heartstrings, and said that he couldn't live without drinking. I felt deeply sorry for him, but I decided that night that I must be strong.

It was time to make a completely fresh start, with no ties. And no more heartache. After that day, I made a vow to myself to limit contact with Adam to just speaking about the children. I tried to move on with my life and he moved on with his. It needed to be this way otherwise we would have carried on in that endless cycle of hurt.

And in a period of real change, I decided to start a small business from home as a bookkeeper, setting up a little home office in the spare room. Work was slow to come in, but eventually it got off the ground. Choosing my own hours is perfect for me and I am very disciplined, so the business has thrived. Friends often say that they think I should go out to work in an office so that I can socialise more, but I am happy with my lot.

The actual house has been a pleasant surprise. The exterior looked drab to me initially, but I painted the front door white, and placed two pots containing six-foot-tall Italian Cypress trees either side. More importantly, the interior has a nice feel.

It is true that I have tended towards social isolation recently, as I just feel tired and not particularly inclined to socialise. When Adam and I first parted, I had got close to a group of local women, some of whom I am still in contact with. For about six months, I had quite a wild time, with lots of nights out and lots of dalliances with men, but nothing serious. But I can honestly say that my more sedate lifestyle now just feels right.

I also tried online dating back then and initially found it quite exciting. I would crack open a bottle of wine and settle in at the computer for a few hours in the evening. I tended to get passionately involved very quickly, and then to get disappointed and disillusioned just as quickly. I was transported back to being a young woman again, tied to the phone waiting around, doubting myself, albeit a mobile phone as opposed to a wall mounted chunky rotary dial phone.

Maybe it was the type of man I was going for, but none of them were entirely honest to me, to varying degrees. One guy I met up with didn't drive, so I drove an hour to meet him, and, during the evening, I crashed my car. The guy, who had previously been so complimentary and lovely, was so pathetic and unhelpful; it was the final straw for me.

Around the time, I got back into listening to my music, my passion for both love and music revived. Dating and heartache always seem to go hand in hand with music, and when I am not dating or in love, I tend to avoid it. I remember playing Tinie Tempah's 'Pass Out' over and over during that time. The words to the song weren't of consequence to me, it was the uplifting beat that got me.

Relationship life cycles were condensed into two weeks, a month at most, a constant rollercoaster of self-confidence and self-doubt, but the continual disappointments took their toll and I eventually removed myself from the dating site. Inviting heartbreak back into my life was just not worth it. That was my last foray into online dating.

For now, I am happily single and, apart from my nocturnal terrors, I am content. Although I have been experiencing horrendous dreams, last night I had a beautiful, comforting dream featuring my grandma.

I am walking along a long winding narrow grey path on my own and I think of the yellow brick road from *The Wizard of Oz*. I feel happy as I can see Adam further down the road, ahead of me. As I get closer to him, I realise that he looks sad, and he isn't saying anything, just watching me approach. I feel a rush of emotion for him, a need mixed with sorrow.

I walk faster to reach him to give him comfort but as I get closer, I can faintly hear someone behind me, calling my name. I look back and see my grandma, standing at a fork in the road, with her friend Lena, who died a few years ago. Lena was always a bit stand-offish in life, so I am not surprised when she just kind of nods at me in acknowledgment and turns back to Grandma, who waves at me and then continues to talk to Lena.

I look back at Adam, who is still waiting for me. I am torn, but I must go and see Grandma. When I reach her, Lena has now disappeared and I say, 'Grandma, you're here!'

She smiles but doesn't reply and then takes me by the hand and leads me away from the path I was on and takes me in the opposite direction, down another path.

My lovely grandma died a month ago, aged ninety-nine, but I truly feel like she is with me, trying to guide me.

I do look back fondly at the secret relationship between Adam and me, which was sadly doomed to failure. I seem to be a self-saboteur, jumping into relationships knowing from the outset that they will fail. I heard recently that Adam was seeing a woman from his local. I've told the children that I don't wany any details, as I'd rather not know. They see their dad regularly and I am happy that they have maintained a close relationship with him.

Darcy met her boyfriend, Rhyder, when she was eighteen and they moved in together just over a year ago. She works as a trainee mental health counsellor. Darcy absolutely loves her job, and she was born to help people. I'm hoping that someday she may be able to do some work on her mum.

Billy is still living at home, working as a self-employed plasterer, arriving home each day in the late afternoon, looking exhausted, covered in plaster. He is a drinker, like his dad, but he is still young, and I hope he doesn't become reliant upon alcohol. I try to talk to him about it occasionally, but he is a young adult now and thinks he knows better.

Both the children have grown into lovely young adults and I am so relieved that all the teenage angst has passed. They don't seem to have been too adversely affected by my split with Adam. Darcy has admitted that she prefers us being apart, as she could sense we were unhappy together, added to the fact that she likes the double Christmas and birthday celebrations, not to mention gifts. Billy doesn't say much, but I would say that the breakup affected him more as he is slightly more sensitive than Darcy.

Last month, along with the extended family, we celebrated Darcy and Billy's 21st birthday at a beautiful Italian restaurant in London, and afterwards, they went off to a club in Soho with a group of friends. Adam had turned up to the restaurant late, predictably drunk already, being overexuberant and loud. I just find him embarrassing and a bit pathetic now. And I feel sad for him.

Adam rarely enters my dreams and I have always wondered about this. Is it because he's not a key player in my life's journey? He has certainly inhabited a large chunk of my life. But last night's dream still nags at me. I felt a deep pull towards him, to at least comfort him, but Grandma was leading me away.

It is easy to work out that my dream indicates my need to move on and not weaken, to live my own life. If only it were so easy to decipher my nightmares and, especially, my nighttime visits. If it weren't for the night terrors, my life would be as I want it to be.

I need to put an end to this, somehow.

4

With the advance of information on the net, I begin to search for answers online. Sitting at my work desk, I look out at the spring bulbs poking through the earth, the cherry tree already in blossom, the pale blue sky filling me with calm. I feel that familiar urge to get out in the garden and start readying the area for summer. Hours spent weeding and pruning are some of my most carefree but before I allow myself that pleasure, my puzzle needs delving into further.

I start by searching online for night terrors, but the results refer to standard nightmares. Interestingly, I find that the word "mare", from "nightmare", is an old English word meaning an oppressive spirit. I then tap in "night paralysis". "Night paralysis demon" appears as a search option in my browser and sparks my interest. I click on the link and read through an article entitled 'Sleep Paralysis Demon: What's Really Going on Here?'

The article describes an imaginary nighttime demon caused by waking up during the dream phase of sleep, with the bodily paralysis caused by the brain turning off signals to the rest of the body to prevent it from acting out dreams. Also explained in the same article is lucid dreaming, where you can take control of your dream because you are aware of your consciousness. Lucid dreaming is a common occurrence for me. I find these dreams enjoyable in the main, even if they are what are commonly known as nightmares. Having control of the situation changes the entire arc of the dream. Sleep paralysis does fit very closely with my experience, but I know in my heart that my visitor is a real entity.

The longer I surf the internet, the more I see how common the nighttime demon is in cultures and countries all over the world. My online research has, at least, elicited two conclusions that fit with my experiences, sleep paralysis and, the one that I feel in my heart of hearts is a fit, the incubus/succubus theory.

The demons are said to torment women in the male form of an incubus and men in the female form of a succubus. Although the scientific explanation points towards sleep paralysis, it is not treatable as such, aside from ensuring you have enough rest and have a good bedtime routine. Despite attempts by scientists to explain the phenomenon, my research found that it is little understood.

I have always thought of myself as a good sleeper. This is bizarre, given the nature of my sleep. I cannot remember ever having experienced a sleepless night, and I fall asleep very soon after my head hits the pillow.

I have never been what you would call scientifically minded. The supernatural has held a lifelong fascination for me and this is perhaps because the house that I grew up in was a former care home for the elderly and I experienced many strange, unexplained events during my childhood and teenage years. From unexplained footsteps in an empty house to half-heard whispers and unexplained draughts of icy air, I accepted the unusual activity and went about my business. But when I moved to new homes throughout the years, the activity followed me.

5

I decide to take my mind off demons and nightmares, as
my imagination is running riot. This can't be healthy. I
decide to cook something nice for Billy and me tonight,
so I head to Sainsbury's to stock up on groceries.

The supermarket is not as busy as usual, making
shopping a more enjoyable chore. I walk along the
central aisle, setting aside thoughts of my internet
discoveries, pushing my nearly empty trolley, and
glance down an aisle without turning in. I stop, my heart
hammering hard, and everything seems to go in slow
motion. There is complete, deathly silence. The only
sound is the rushing of blood in my ears.

Halfway down the aisle on the left there is a dark
grey mass looking as if it is climbing the shelf. The
horror of looking at it is palpable. The mass becomes
more solid and there he is, the incubus, with an evil,
mocking grin on his face. My hands let go of the trolley,
which rolls away on its own, leaving me standing like a
deer in the headlights. I freeze and, within what must be
a matter of seconds, the apparition disappears. My
mouth is dry as a bone and I stare stupidly at the spot
where the visitor was.

I register an elderly lady from the corner of my vision, and she shuffles over and lays her hand on my forearm, 'Are you okay?' I look at the kind-faced woman and feel alternately hot and cold, as I mutter, 'Yes, sorry, um, I'm fine... I'm not well,' and I turn to find my trolley.

Back in the car, although the fear is much dissipated, I still feel its residue. I realise that the shape of the creature I saw was an exact replica of what I had seen when researching online, down to the crouching position and the evil smile on its face. I had clearly overdone it with the research and my exhausted mind had manifested this vision.

You need to get some rest! I lecture myself and I activate a playlist on my music app for the drive home, selecting shuffle. The first song that comes on is 'See You in My Nightmares', a haunting song by Kanye West.

As he sings 'I got the right to put up a fight, but not quite, 'cause you cut off my light,' I think, *this is taking over my life now.*

6

Saturday afternoon, the day after the incident in the supermarket, I spend perhaps too much time in my own head trying to solve the mystery. A nagging thought, although unpleasant, of something that perhaps needs exploring is regression therapy. I know Layla has an interest in this subject, so I call her.

'I would love to go for that,' confirms Layla. Her interest is for a different reason to mine, though. Layla is keen to find out if she has lived a past life. 'I couldn't care less about past lives,' I say, and we joke about who we think she may have been, ranging from Audrey Hepburn to Genghis Khan. We agree to find a practitioner online.

'Anyway, come over for a catch-up. Si is here but he'll make himself scarce.' I had been hoping she would invite me over. Although I like Si, we can't really be ourselves and talk in-depth in front of him. But I want to see her, so I get myself ready and head over.

Pulling into Layla's road, I glance to my left, as I always do, at a gorgeous, thatched cottage set just off the road. Layla lives in what we refer to as the 'sticks', which seems an unfair nickname for this beautiful countryside.

Driving here in the spring is particularly lovely, tiny villages with a profusion of spring bulbs on every grass area available, clearly competing with their neighbouring village to our advantage. I never tire of the approach to Layla's cottage. Set in a row of stone-built cottages on the tiny high street, the whole front, up to the guttering, is covered in ivy which has been neatly removed in a straight line from the adjoining neighbours. This always strikes me as comical, as I can imagine the neighbours peeping out of their windows continually looking for one ivy leaf threatening their precious façade. The front door porch area juts out and is set on a right angle.

Layla answers the door looking lovely as usual. I have never seen her look anything other than stylish and well groomed. We air kiss in our exaggerated fashion.

We go through to the airy, light-filled front room and sit beside each other on her gorgeous chunky wooden bench adorned with nautical-themed pillows, behind a coffee table laden with coffee and biscuits. With oak wooden beams throughout and small doors, the cottage is so full of character. I mentally note a few small décor touches that I would like to recreate at home, including a feature wall with gorgeous cream and blue damask wallpaper.

The incredible voice of Whitney Houston is belting from the Bose sound system, sounding particularly poignant following the recent news of her death.

'Let's hear, then,' says Layla, as I take my mobile phone out of my bag. I access the sleep app that I downloaded to investigate my quality of sleep and, hope of hopes, to see whether there are any strange noises recorded. We play back the recordings. My heart jumps when I first hear myself talking in my sleep and we rewind each sound and listen back with the sound cranked up. Some nonsensical rantings, but nothing I could connect with my visitor. We laugh at my nocturnal chatting and I find myself thinking how nice that I can share this with a friend, as it makes the situation much more light-hearted.

The most surprising finding from the app's recordings is how little I am asleep at night. The app shows dashes when the person is asleep, and it seems that last night's sleep involved me waking forty-three times. This is a shock, as I had always thought that I was a good sleeper. No wonder I am exhausted and starting to hallucinate about demons in supermarkets.

7

Late afternoon, and Layla persuades me to stay for dinner. Si organises a M & S ready meal, a Chinese stir fry dish accompanied with crisp, dry white wine. He has even placed candles on the table, which is a nice touch. All right, no cutlery, but he tried his best. I think of Adam, who had never prepared me even a slice of toast and think how lucky Layla is in some ways.

We chat and laugh until it is dark outside and talk turns to alternative therapies. I'm surprised to learn that Si has recently trained in Reiki healing. I agree to an aura "reading", not thinking too much other than that this should be fun, but I have drunk a bit too much wine.

Si asks me to sit on a straight-backed chair and he steps behind me to begin the process. He places his hands about ten inches on either side of my head and I instantly sense his reservations.

He is silent for minutes, and then says, 'Ooh, wow, I can't do this.' Silence for a few seconds.

'What's up?' asks Layla.

'It's probably nothing, but your aura feels dark and not friendly... I literally can't get near you.' He backs away, perhaps without realising and looks embarrassed, but I try to make a joke of it to save his blushes.

'Ah, not to worry, I always knew I was demonic,' I say. Layla joins in, as she picks up on the awkwardness of the situation.

'At least look for 666 on her head, Si,' she says, and we all laugh. I think briefly of Layla's mum's comment about me having a dark cloud over me, all those years ago. Si must feel a similar way.

Layla then rapidly changes the subject, jumping in there, as good friends do.

'Si, our glasses are empty…' Si smiles, relieved, and goes off in search of more wine.

Subject closed, we carry on with the evening.

I am now well over the limit thanks to the endless glasses of wine, so I decide to stay over rather than get a cab and leave my car. Leading me up to her spare room, Layla and I laugh about the evening and, in particular, Si's fear when he tried to "heal" me. I always gently rib Si, but he knows I am fond of him. At the top of the stairs there is an arched wooden-framed mirror and I see that my eye make-up has smudged on to my face from all the laughing.

The spare room is as stylish as the rest of Layla's home, with dark but vibrant blue walls, a chevron patterned blind, and a few lovely shabby chic ornaments dotted around the wooden furniture. The single wooden wardrobe has been distressed with white paint and a gold rub. I take everything in but briefly, as I need some sleep.

After getting ready for bed, involving just a borrowed toothbrush and a long t-shirt from Layla, I lie back on the comfy bed in Layla's spare room and put my mobile phone playlist on shuffle, quietly, so as not to disturb Layla and Si.

Runaway by Kanye West is the song that pops up. 'Baby, I got a plan, run away as fast as you can… Run away from me baby, run away'…

I am trying I think, but you won't let me.

2011

2010

2009

2008

2007

2006

PART THREE
35 YEARS OLD

2005 – 14 years ago
1

I am with Mandy in a posh-looking kitchen showroom. It's not a place that I've been before. The space is huge with incredibly high ceilings like an aircraft hangar. Beautiful kitchens are spread over the entire floor area and we can't see anyone else there, no staff, no customers. We come across a gorgeous show kitchen with black shiny worktops, and I notice that there is a chunky catalogue placed on the kitchen island. I pick it up and start to flick through, but it is entirely blank. This must be a printing error. Who would leave a blank catalogue out for customers to look through? Mandy and I check out more kitchen displays, and on one worktop there is a plate of pretty cupcakes. We check that no staff members are within sight, and then we start to shovel the cakes in, gorging ourselves. We manage to finish the entire plate and then run out of the showroom, laughing,

I notice that I am wearing jeans that are so tight for me that they have split up the front of the legs, from the ankle to the crotch, and they are now just swaying flaps of material. Layla has disappeared, and I am walking in the back door of a house which is a cross between my childhood home and my current home.

I wander through the kitchen, which is much larger than mine, and go into the hallway. No one seems to be in the house with me, but then I open a door to my left and see Adam sitting on his own on a straight-backed kitchen chair in the centre of a room, his head hanging down. Apart from a matching chair directly in front of Adam, the rest of the room is completely bare, no furniture, not a single item. I realise that the chair is for me to sit on, and he has been waiting for me. Adam doesn't look up as I enter and take a seat, so he seemed to be expecting me.

Once I am opposite Adam, we look at each other and start to quietly, calmly, discuss arrangements for our parting of ways and I get a real sense of sadness, almost grief.

I wake up and feel that aching sadness that seems, somehow, worse in a dream. I must go back to sleep to try to make everything better. I start to plan the dream and try to will myself to drift off again.

I find myself standing halfway up a small hill which I somehow know is in Hampstead. I'm disappointed that I'm not back in the dream with Adam, but maybe I can twist this dream to suit me. It is nighttime and I notice the passing car's headlights flash by as I stand still, looking up the hill. I feel that I might be invisible.

Slightly further up, nearly at the crest of the hill, I see a small group of young men, in their early twenties, huddled together, heads down, talking in hushed tones. I somehow know that I am not supposed to be watching them and they don't know that I am here. Whatever their nighttime meeting is about, it feels furtive and unpleasant, like something bad is being planned. Three of the men are Asian, and the fourth young man is of Jamaican or African heritage, with a short afro.

I walk closer, feeling nervous, as I'm not sure whether I will remain invisible. They are speaking quietly but urgently and seem to be plotting and planning. I can't hear what they are saying but something is wrong.

Then an ambulance pulls up, lights flashing, and the paramedics load the man with the short afro on to a stretcher and take him away. Somehow, I know that he is being taken to St Thomas' Hospital in London.

I wake up feeling confused and disappointed, I want to continue this dream and find out what is going on. What were the men plotting? It felt like one of my psychic dreams in that it has imprinted on my mind and feels symbolic somehow. I will be scanning the newspapers tomorrow to see if there is a match, and I have no doubt that something will crop up.

It felt so real, but I just couldn't hear what they were saying. And what if I could? What if I heard every single word and it made sense? I can hardly call 999 and say that I think three Asian men and a black man are going to commit a crime but I'm sorry, I have no idea what that crime is.

'Where did you get your information, madam?' the police phone operator would say.

'I dreamt it,' would be my pathetic reply.

The operator would be rolling their eyes and drawing a huge circle in the air next to their head, to the amusement of their colleagues.

No, that won't be happening. But I am still intrigued. I try to go back to sleep to get back into the dream.

I start to feel drowsy, and then I start to hear, and then feel, that old familiar radio static in my mind. Memories of past visits flash into my mind. I realise that Adam is lying asleep next to me as I can feel his back on my right arm and I also feel the vibration on the bed of his slow breathing.

I don't remember the visitor ever coming in the night when someone else was in the bed with me. Will Adam feel anything or sense anything? It is not a thought that brings much hope as Adam sleeps like the dead. I always joke that I would have to fight off a burglar and he would sleep through it. How can I get his attention? But then, what could he do, even if he does wake up? He may look over at me and think I am having some type of medical emergency, a heart attack or stroke.

Then comes the familiar weight on the bed. A horse-racing commentator's opening gambit randomly pops into my head, 'Aaaaand... we're off!'

My feet are quickly uncovered, weight on my legs, my chest, my wrists... Keep your eyes closed tight... Wake up Adam! I try to shout. With all my effort, I try to speak and all I can muster is a barely audible drugged-sounding slur. I strain my right arm, but it is a dead weight, no movement at all. I am completely paralysed.

He's back.

2

Monday morning, still dark outside, I lie in bed, last night's dream nagging at me. I can feel Adam beside me, stirring. I have come to dislike even his touch, however accidental. Our relationship feels like it is in its dying stages and all I can feel is irritation and, beyond that, hope that this will soon be over.

I glance around at the bedroom that I have spent so much time and effort decorating. I have decorated from scratch and it does look exactly how I imagined it to. Teal-coloured walls, cream soft furnishings and oak furniture, with a gorgeous chandelier to finish off the room. The chandelier is way too grand for our tiny home, but I don't care. I will miss the look of the room, but it is easy enough to start again, and everything but the walls can come with me when I leave.

Vestiges of last night's dream and then the visit come back to me and the thoughts are abruptly interrupted by Adam's radio alarm clock, which makes my heart jump. The sounds of Green Day's 'Boulevard of Broken Dreams' blasts out.

"I walk a lonely road, the only one that I have ever known,

don't know where it goes, but it's home to me, and I walk alone.'

The music is way too loud for this time of the morning. Adam groans, mumbles something incoherent and switches the alarm off. He then gets up, in his angry way. No conversation, no 'Morning' as couples always seem to say in the films, nothing.

We have both, in our own ways, tried to make things work. But old wounds just won't heal, and we are stuck in an unhealthy situation where we are punishing each other in a never-ending cycle.

I try to think of the good times and the positives. We used to laugh together so much at the beginning. We still, on occasion, laugh together. But the odd joke in no way indicates any strengthening of our broken relationship.

We have two beautiful children, so I don't regret meeting Adam, but I wish I had gone it alone. But then, if I had, the children's relationship with Adam may not have been as close.

He is a lovely dad, I will never take that away from him. I need to be thankful for that and to try to push all negative thoughts about his infidelity and drinking problem to the special storage box in my brain. But it is difficult to do.

As I hear Adam in the bathroom, going about his morning routine, I allow myself to fantasise about not having to listen to him again, having the bed to myself, more cupboard space, the list goes on. There are no negatives that I can think of, apart from the financial side. And I am thirty-five, which is young enough to start again, if I decide to. Will I be sad when it's over? Yes, but only for the children.

And for what could have been but never was.

3

Monday morning, back in the old routine. I like to walk the children part way to their school, so that I can grab the paper from the corner shop. They wouldn't dream of letting me walk them all the way, which is understandable as they are teenagers. However, they don't say no to a lift if I am taking the car.

Arriving home, I glance at the newspaper and notice the date: 7th July. The number 7 attracts my attention as it always does, and I decide to scan the paper thoroughly later.

More importantly, I call my grandma on the house phone. Although I now have a nice new Nokia mobile phone, Grandma certainly doesn't have a mobile, so I always seem to go the traditional route when calling her. With my parents away on holiday, I take the reins and call Grandma regularly, both morning and evening, to check on her and encourage her to take her tablets.

I have such a close bond with Grandma. I have always asked her advice on anything and everything and all her advice has resonated with me, even if I haven't always taken it.

She is now reaching the age where she is beginning to show signs of Alzheimer's, which saddens me so much. Such a vibrant, intelligent woman, I sense that she will struggle with this awful degenerative disease.

Grandma answers the phone, as she always does, by saying her entire telephone number, complete with area code, very slowly. As she says it, I smile and think that I am relieved that she still remembers it. I feel a pang of sorrow as I imagine the day will soon come when she no longer remembers the number.

'Hello, darling.'

Grandma's warm greeting never fails to touch me. We chat for a while, getting the practicalities out of the way, ensuring she has taken her pills and eaten properly.

Whilst chatting, I say, 'Grandma, can I ask, have I got any connection with St Thomas' Hospital?'

'No, darling, not that I'm aware of.'

'Ah, okay. Do you know where it is?'

'Yes,' she replies, 'It's next to the Thames, over Westminster Bridge Road. I visited your Aunty Joan there years and years ago when she was in that car accident. Why do you ask?'

'Ah, just one of those weird dreams, and someone in the dream was taken to that particular hospital.'

Grandma doesn't have time to reply as she suddenly says, 'Oh my goodness, have you got the TV on? There's been some type of serious incident in London!'

I said I hadn't, said I would call her back and dashed into the front room to switch on the TV and flick through to the news.

4

Watching the news footage on BBC One, I sit down heavily on the sofa and watch the tragedy unfold with horror. As the events are uncovered, it is quickly determined that a terror attack has been carried out in London, confirmed mid-morning by the Home Secretary. With the children due to be picked up from school by Adam later, as he is taking them to buy new sports kits for school, I watch the streaming, flicking between BBC One and ITV, nearly all day.

Although initially it had been reported that power surges were causing the explosions, it was discovered that four suicide bombers – three Asian and one of Jamaican heritage – carried out the attack on the London Underground and a double decker bus nearby. Three of the bombs went off on trains at 8.49 a.m., and a fourth bomb was detonated on the bus at 9.47 a.m.

It is heart-breaking watching the panic and sorrow on screen.

A total of fifty-six people, including the four bombers, died and more than seven hundred were injured.

My interest is drawn to the bomber of Jamaican heritage, Germaine Lindsay, who, in my dream, had been taken to St Thomas' Hospital on a stretcher. As it happens, reports confirm that he had died at the scene of the bombing. St Thomas' Hospital did treat twenty people following the attack, but the Royal London Hospital treated most victims.

The elements of my dream repeat themselves time and again whilst watching the news. The plotting together, the nationality of the men, but in particular the specifics of the one man that stood out. I don't claim to know the answers. I only wish I did.

My dreams usually foretell what I consider to be mundane events surrounding me in my daily life, but on occasion I dream of big disasters prior to them happening. The details of the dreams are never clear enough for me to pinpoint exactly what will happen, let alone where, as I only get a snippet, so I'm never going to be able to prevent anything from happening.

But I believe that my dreams can guide me on a personal level, so for now I must make the most of that and continue to note down my dreams.

What I can't even begin to get my head around is why I foresaw some crucial details of this incident. It makes no sense to me. I have no real connection to Hampstead, no connection at all with terror, or religion, no connection with anyone involved—the perpetrators or, indeed, the victims, as far as I am aware.

Although I sometimes dream of catastrophic events that come true, there seems to be no rhyme nor reason for this one. All I can think is that I foresee what will occur in the next day or two of my life, be that personal incidents or news items that I am glued to.

And then I remember the date. 7th July.

7th of the 7th.

5

Saturday, mid-morning, Adam parks the car near to the beach on the Southend seafront, all of us relieved to have arrived on this hot, sunny day. This weekend we have decided to bring the children to the coast for a day trip.

Getting out of the car is a sweet relief for us all, emerging to the sound of seagulls, the calming sway of the ocean, the smells of ocean air, candy floss and fish and chips.

We laugh at how large and bold the seagulls are, 'Seagulls on steroids,' says Adam. Unfortunately, that is practically his quota of words for the day.

At lunchtime, we sit outside around a wooden table in the garden of a pub near the front, having finished a nice traditional fish and chips. The children seem happy enough, Darcy playing a game on my phone and Billy playing a game on Adam's phone. Due to their age, they are generally quite sullen, but the sea air seems to have perked them up.

Now teenagers, until Darcy and Billy were around eleven years of age, they were completely content spending most of their time together. I tried to encourage friendships for both and, although we had many children over to play throughout the years, any friends invariably felt left out as Darcy and Billy had such an easy bond. But when the hormones started to kick in, Darcy began to spend more time alone, and Billy just didn't understand why. They now have their own groups of friends, some mutual, and I feel that this is healthier for them as I never wanted them to be too dependent on one another.

The sun is blazing in the sky and younger children are playing on the swings and wooden treehouse and slide nearby, having a great time. The table nearest to us is in direct opposition to ours, in that the family are laughing, being tactile and chatting happily. To illustrate the point, the woman whom I identify as the mother of the group laughs loudly and kisses the smiling man to her right. They are even sitting next to each other, I think, feeling jealousy rear its head.

In contrast, Adam sips his beer with an angry look on his face. I don't want to get into an argument today, but I am so tempted to say, 'For God's sake, cheer up!' Can't he see that other people are happy to be at the seaside with their families? I don't notice any of the music coming from the speakers directly outside the back doors of the pub, until the opening bars of Mr Brightside by The Killers.

"Jealousy, turning saints into the sea
Swimming through sick lullabies, choking on your alibis

But it's just the price I pay, destiny is calling me
Open my eager eyes, 'cause I'm Mr. Brightside"

Adam and I glance at each other and something passes between us. This is one song that we both like but sadly one song does not a relationship make.

Something about the song reminds me of last week's nocturnal visit. Surprisingly, I haven't thought about the visit since, probably because I have been so busy with the children and just life in general. My visitor came to me even though Adam was lying next to me. Can even the visitor feel that there is nothing left for me inside Adam's cold heart? And vice versa.

I have been thinking for a while that, rather than let Adam and his coldness take up my head space, I need to delve further into the nocturnal visits. I think back to my childhood and wonder whether there could be any answers there.

Had my mum taken me to the doctors for more than just nightmares? I know I used to sleepwalk and I regularly woke up screaming. I need to try every avenue. It's then that I decide that I will ask my doctor for access to my medical records.

I need to figure this out.

6

On my way back from picking up the paper, I try out my new iPod shuffle with its little earphones. I love this tiny object. It seems that the more distanced I become from Adam, the more that I am getting back into my music. I listen to the easy rhythm of Mario singing 'Let me Love You'.

Soon after I get home and grab a coffee, I call the doctors' surgery to make an appointment. I make a request with the receptionist to access my medical records and my doctor calls back within the hour. He confirms that I can pop in now as a member of staff happens to be available to sit with me, which is a requirement when accessing a doctor's notes. I thank him and head over.

I manage to get a parking space directly outside the surgery. As I get out of the car and walk to the entrance, I can smell the gorgeous garlic aroma from a local restaurant preparing for lunchtime service, the summer heat making the smell pungent and reminiscent of holidays abroad. Under the circumstances that Adam and I are in, we won't be going on holiday overseas for the foreseeable future.

Holidays were the only time that we were truly happy. I think back to our adventures on our various holidays over the years. We were happy for two weeks a year, and miserable for the remaining fifty weeks.

Inside the waiting room, following a short wait, Jenna, whom I had previously worked with at the surgery, comes to get me. As she leads me to the room that we will be spending the next hour in together, we catch up. I am fond of Jenna, which makes the experience pleasant as opposed to tense. She hands me the buff coloured A5 patient file, and I feel an initial nervous rush. Then, flicking through the papers in descending order, from my most recent visit, and taking snaps of every note in the file going way back to my birth, I feel relieved that I had remembered to fully charge my phone.

Wow, I think, I've got some work to do.

That evening, settling in at my kitchen table, the children in their bedrooms and Adam out goodness knows where, I access the photo app on my phone. I then start the arduous task of trying to decipher the doctor's scribbled writing, not to mention the medical terms and codes, which I manage to solve with the help of Google. I had worked for a boss many years ago whose handwriting was barely legible, giving me a bit of an advantage with this task. I am nothing if not determined.

Slowly, but surely, I decode about 95% of the wording. Ultimately, everything about my medical history is standard and there are no surprises. Apart from a visit to the doctors (when I was seven) for nightmares, where the doctor in question had recommended limiting my time watching television, my file consists of the standard sore throats and coughs and colds. But nothing of note.

I am content that I have this particular box ticked and feel a sense of relief.

What next?

7

Saturday night, feeling good, dressed in skinny jeans, a white vest and white wooden wedge heels, with my hair straightened, I arrive at Natalie's house for her 40th birthday party. Getting these jeans over my hips earlier on had taken an enormous effort with no blood, but certainly sweat and tears.

As I approach the front door, I hear loud music and lots of voices and laughing, and I feel relieved that I am fashionably late. Natalie answers the door after a minute or so and I hand over a bottle of wine and a bunch of flowers.

'Look at you!' says Natalie, looking surprised as she looks me up and down, holding my arm, and I smile.

'And look at you!' She looks great, with her hair straightened and styled like Rachel from *Friends*. Natalie is a fellow mum from the children's school, so we usually see each other perhaps not looking our best, and this is our first time together in a social setting away from the school gates. We catch up and then drift apart as we spot others.

Natalie's house is nondescript from the outside but deceptive, as the décor inside is stylish and expensive looking, with lots of old wooden furniture and gorgeous soft furnishings.

I spot a friend, Mandy.

'Hello lovely,' she says, and we air kiss each other in a jokey way.

'Quick!' She leads me to the huge marble-topped kitchen island, which is covered in food and drink of every variety.

'Get one of these before they go,' she says, grabbing a frosted pastel-coloured cupcake for herself, and I follow her lead. My dream of gorging on cupcakes comes back to me briefly, but I set it aside. We have a catch-up and ooh and aah over the food that Natalie's daughter had organised. We giggle at the boxed wine, labelled "Good White Wine".

'It must be good, it says so on the box.'

As the party goes on, the music coming from the stereo is getting everyone in the mood, and I smile at a younger group I don't know in the corner, all of them wearing velour Juicy Couture tracksuits and doing a silly Beyonce-style dance to Amerie's '1 Thing'. I'm never one to dance but I love to watch others.

Feeling good, as one of my favourite old songs comes on, Fat Joe's 'What's Luv?', I stand chatting to James, an old work mate. We catch up on local gossip, then James starts to talk about the London bombings. He refers to them as the '7/7' bombings, as they were carried out on the 7th day of the 7th month. This is the first time I have heard the incident referred to in this way.

All the 7s.

I head off at around eleven p.m., jumping in a cab. Desperate to get these suffocating jeans off and get ready for bed, I'm relieved when I put my key in the door. But as soon as I open the front door slightly, I can smell the strong odour of cannabis.

Whenever I go out, which is not that often, Adam takes the opportunity to smoke cannabis in the house, which he knows I hate. The children are at such an impressionable age, and I don't doubt that they know what the smell is.

As I approach the table where he is sitting, listening to his music on a CD player and puffing on his joint, he doesn't look up. I try to bite my tongue, but I can't.

We start to argue and at one point, Adam blames his drinking problem on me. But even as he says it, he looks vaguely embarrassed. I have a tendency to go below the belt when arguing with Adam and, sure enough, I blurt out that I find him 'pathetic' and 'a loser'.

Our argument goes on into the early morning, in partially hushed tones so as not to wake the children. But the hushed tones somehow make it worse, the words seeming more deadly. By 2.45 a.m., we agree to split for good.

This has been a long time coming. For years now we have been arguing and have had next to no interests, groups of friends or even likes/dislikes in common.

Our one commonality is the children, and we have always been attracted to one another. I wish this weren't the case, it certainly complicates things. Why could I have not had chemistry with a kind, caring man?

Although I drank at the party, and Adam had a drink and a smoke, we are sober by the time the protracted argument reaches its closing stages. Towards the end, we soften towards one another when discussing arrangements going forward. To his credit, Adam wants the break-up to be as amicable as possible to save the children extra heartache, which I wholeheartedly agree with. If we can pull this parting of ways off, that would be one good thing that we have achieved together.

A twelve-year relationship is over. Twelve years that never should have happened, but I can't feel regret because of our two wonderful children.

My grandma had once described relationships as two people working together towards a common goal, supporting one another. Whereas Adam and I have ended up as two strangers with children in common, living in the same house, unhappily. I feel sad, but relieved.

Onwards and upwards.

2004

2003

2002

2001
2000
1999

PART FOUR
28 YEARS OLD

1998 – 21 years ago
1

I am slowly working my way around the ground floor of a huge abandoned-looking house that I don't feel like I have been in before. The large, spacious rooms have barely any furniture and horribly grimy windows. The house is badly run-down, with wallpaper peeling off, and huge chunks of plaster crumbling from areas of the walls and ceilings.

There are squatters dotted about in some of the rooms who don't seem to be taking any notice of me. They all seem a bit gloomy and sad-eyed, all with bald heads and grey skin. They are mostly clustered in corners, talking amongst themselves quietly and completely oblivious to me. I feel like I am entirely invisible to them or maybe they should be invisible to me. I can't work out which.

I then hear heavy footsteps echoing through the house, coming for me, sounding like heavy boots walking on wooden floorboards, but amplified. The sound is ominous, and I know whoever or whatever is hunting me is bad.

I start to feel panic rising, and I look this way and that, running from room to room, trying to find a hiding place, but not knowing the house. There is very little furniture, so no wardrobes to hide in. I decide on trying to reach the roof, as he or it won't be able to follow me out there.

I get the feeling that the man, or beast, or animal can't go outside, so the roof will be a perfect place for me to get to. Where are Darcy and Billy? I feel that they are not here with me, they are somewhere else.

The squatters don't seem to be bothered by the footsteps, which somehow scares me more. Are they used to someone being hunted while they go about their business? To be so blasé about it must mean it is a common occurrence, and it also means that they won't be any help at all. A telephone starts to ring loudly and that is also being ignored by the squatters. Shall I pick it up? No, I think it is somehow connected. It might be a trick.

I run up a flight of stairs, and then another and another, how big is this house? I get to the top of one flight of stairs, and there is a small window with bright light beaming in. The window doesn't look big enough to climb through and I am terrified of getting stuck, but I stop at the window for a break, to catch my breath.

I look down and see a red mobile phone on the window ledge. This is Adam's phone; what is it doing here? Has he been here? Is he here now? I pick up the phone and the display has the name Lesley on it. So, Lesley has been phoning him.

That horrible feeling of betrayal eats me up, again, tugging at my heart. I wonder if they are in this house. I am torn between running from the predator who is chasing me and looking for Adam and Lesley to catch them in the act. Either way, I need to get moving.

I begin to climb the stairs again, continuing to run upwards. What if this never ends? I finally end up in a room on the top floor that has neon lights all over the walls. The room feels nicer, safer than the rest of the house. I know that I need to get to the window at the far side of the room which leads to the roof. But there is a huge puddle in the middle of the floor, and I sense that it is very deep. Quick, think! He's coming!

I end up running quickly and as lightly as possible over the water, almost skimming the surface, and reach the window. On the window ledge there is a pile of neatly placed light bulbs, all lit up but not plugged into any electrical source. Water and electricity don't mix, I think; I will get electrocuted. So, I grasp about on the grimy floor for something that I can use to smash the bulbs, being mindful of getting water on my hands. My hand closes around a mallet, what I imagine is a croquet mallet, and I smash every single bulb until they are just small shards of glass.

I turn back, to see whether the entity chasing me is in the room yet, and I see that there is a central ceiling bulb hanging down, also lit, but I know I can't reach it with the mallet. If I fall in the water and the bulb smashes, it could kill me, I'm sure. My chances of skimming over the water again and trying to reach it are slim, and I don't want to push my luck.

Over in the far-right corner of the room, across the stretch of water, I see a little boy of about seven or eight years old with jet-black hair. He is sitting in a huge chair. I feel like I know him. He's not Billy, as Billy has light-brown hair. How do I know this boy? I feel maternal towards him. He is strapped in by his arms and his ankles. The chair is one of those boxy American electrocution chairs that I've seen in films.

The boy has piercing blue eyes and looks sad. I want to help him but don't know if I can get back across the water to him without drowning. I can't help him, and he seems to realise this. He slowly shakes his head, and his bottom lip is quivering. I am filled with a huge rush of sadness: this poor boy, I can't help him

I wake up with a strong sense of sorrow for the little boy in the chair. Even though I realise that I am now out of the dream, the sorrow is not decreasing. And that huge decrepit house, I wonder if that represents our new home which, though not large, is in need of work. Something is nagging at me and I then relive that bitter feeling of betrayal, as the red mobile phone comes to mind. I don't even need to check Adam's phone; my dream has told me all I need to know. Not so much a symbolic dream, this dream is spelling it out for me. I keep reliving the moment and trying to recreate the full extent of the emotion associated with it. Why do I do that? I have a habit of putting myself back into the emotions of the dreams and seeing if I can feel it, again and again. Self-torture, it seems. Or self-preservation?

I can smell the gloss paint from my DIY session last night. I can see that it is 01:06 a.m., so I've had a few hours of sleep, at least. I am willing the alarm clock not to flash, and I fail.

Oh no, here we go again. I can feel that old sense of dread, which is not dissipating like it should. Move! I can't move. He's on his way... the radio static is loud in my ears and I can see the static in black and white behind my closed eyes. He has followed me to our new home.

Why am I surprised? Did I think he would suddenly disappear? He visited me at our rented flat, so it stands to reason that he would continue to follow me. I try to find a place in my mind that is separate from him, but the static is too loud, and it is making me drowsier. Will he never give up? I'm too tired, I can't fight this.

I can hear Adam's music downstairs, the bass just barely audible. I can almost picture him playing air guitar down there, not a care in the world.

I suddenly have a light-bulb moment. I realise now that part of the paralysis that comes with his visits is sheer exhaustion, whereby my fighting spirit is alive in my mind, but it is too much effort for my body, almost like he is drugging me. I clamp my eyes shut, knowing that I probably won't see anything if I do keep my eyes open, but I'm not taking the risk. Memories of Matt from years ago with his menacing smile come back to me fleetingly.

Eyes closed body tense, paralysis restricting me. Then I feel the weight on the end of the bed. Here you are again. Just get on with it… No, don't! Forget I said that. Stop thinking like that, he will know and may hurt you. I can feel my index finger start to twitch. This is new, I don't remember ever being able to do this before. I keep twitching my finger, in the vain hope that he will think I'm fully awake, but he either doesn't notice or doesn't care. Then the covers come off my feet and that is when I give up. Now that I have given up all efforts to fight, however pathetic they may have been, the only body part that I can feel in motion is the fluttering of my heart in my chest.

2

Opening my eyes, for an instant I don't know where I am. What is that wall? Why isn't my bedroom door there? Then it dawns on me that I am lying in the new bedroom, in our new house.

The room feels very sparse and echoey, with the minimum of furniture or junk. All the boxes containing bedroom items are in the spare room, so all that is furnishing the room now is the bed and wardrobe.

As I glance around the room, the wallpaper irritates me as it always does. The beige, once white, paper is dotted with horrible small blue flowers. The ceiling has a bare bulb and is decorated with woodchip wallpaper which will take a month of Sundays to remove. Even the wardrobe, which we brought with us, needs replacing, but it will have to do for now.

This room will be decorated last as we only sleep in here. The bare floorboards are splattered with old paint from the previous owner's decorating efforts. Not just splatters, in some areas there are whole swathes of smeared paint. It tires me out just looking at it. I feel more tired this morning than I did when I went to bed last night.

I get out of bed to open the window to let some of the paint fumes out. I took the opportunity to paint the skirting boards with gloss paint last night when the children had gone to bed, and the fumes are now permeating the air. Strangely, it's a smell that I like, but I know that it can cause headaches. With the window now open wide, fresh, crisp autumn air flows into the room, neutralising the chemical smell almost immediately.

It is now late September, and we have been at our new home for almost six weeks. Back in September 1991, I gave birth to the twins, Darcy and Billy, so life for the last seven years has been centred around our two little ones. The children have bought such joy to our lives, and the lives of our wider family, especially as they are our parents' first grandchildren.

I found out that I was pregnant when I was already four months gone and it was a complete surprise. I had been putting weight on steadily for a period of a few months, which I put down to depression. My periods had all but stopped, but I hadn't even given that much thought as I have always had irregular cycles, at times two months of freedom and at other times, two periods per month.

I had been getting more emotional than usual and my mum had been the first person to suggest that I needed to at least try a pregnancy test. I didn't think for a moment that I would be pregnant, as I had gone on the pill a week after meeting Adam.

When I had my first scan and was given an estimated birth date, we were able to work out that I had fallen pregnant on my first or second night with Adam. Just my luck. The doctor explained that I had carried "well" as I am tall, as my pregnancy was only obvious in the last trimester. By this time, my tummy was so huge, I felt like a Weeble Wobble.

I clearly remember the evening I walked down to the well woman clinic to have a pregnancy test, so confident that I wasn't pregnant that I popped into the Wine Warehouse on the way and bought a bottle of wine for us to celebrate with when I got home.

When I arrived back at our little rented flat and told Adam the unexpected news, we stared into each other's eyes for a touch too long, as if to say, 'what have we done?' Then, for the rest of the evening, we went through a whole host of emotions, one minute happy, one minute excited, one minute crying, one minute overwhelmed.

At least we felt the same, even if that meant bewildered. The following day, Adam went off the grid, disappearing for the entire day and returning late in the evening. Who he had been with, I don't know, but he had clearly been mulling everything over and making important life decisions. To Adam's credit, he told me that night that he would stand by me through thick and thin and that we were in this together, whatever happened between us.

Even so, my visions for the future at that time had very much been of me as a single mother, and I didn't envisage our relationship being anywhere near strong enough to raise a family together. My mum had been incredibly supportive, and she reassured me that everything would work out fine, but she was in agreement that Adam and I wouldn't last the course. After a few weeks, I got in the spirit of things and started to buy pregnancy magazines and a few baby bits.

During the remainder of my pregnancy, we tried our best to sort our issues out and decided to make a go of it. Adam started to save for a deposit so we could buy our own home as opposed to renting and 'throwing money down the drain' as he put it. The pregnancy continued without any major upsets or setbacks and we were in a good place.

When our beautiful babies came along at the beginning of September, we were so thankful for our happy accident. They became our reason for living. As time went on, I threw myself into the care of the children and took on a part-time job to help with the bills. From the beginning of my pregnancy to the end of May 1993, when the children were two years old, I have only good memories.

Then, in June 1993, I discovered that Adam was seeing Lesley again. The children were with my mum for a couple of days while I temped at my old workplace, a recruitment agency. I was loving the break and enjoying catching up with old workmates. I felt young and free for a brief period.

One afternoon, I left work a couple of hours early as I had a migraine starting. I ordered a cab to take me home, and the cab stopped at the traffic lights in the high street. I glanced over to my right, and I spotted Adam and Lesley, walking together, hand in hand, out of a tiny pub that was an old man's pub. They didn't see me in the cab. They had presumably picked this place as they wouldn't be seen. As the cab was stopped at the red light, my instinct was to jump out and confront them. But I didn't. Somehow, I contained my anger, but I felt physically sick.

I will never forget how I felt that day. The confrontation with Adam that followed was epic and I remember throwing every single item of his personal belongings, including his beloved CD collection, out the front of the house, in the pouring rain.

That period was awful. Following our huge row, Adam moved back in with his mum and slept on her front room floor. Family rallied round me, but I knew I couldn't ever completely come back from this betrayal. I wavered between thinking he had done me a favour and feeling heartbroken. My feelings could literally switch at a moment's notice.

In time, we managed to move towards an amicable place, and, for a while, Adam would come round to babysit at the little flat that we had once shared. I took full advantage of having a reliable babysitter and started to go out with friends in the evenings. I remember enjoying the thrill of getting dressed up to go out and I spent way too much money on new clothes and make-up. I rejoined the gym and got my figure back to my pre-pregnancy weight and I was feeling attractive again. But the new social life began to take over my life, in that I was desperate to get through the days in order to get out at night.

I wanted to hurt Adam, to give him a taste of his own medicine. We were connected through the children and Adam had always sworn that whatever happened between us, he would always be there for the children.

So, I made contact with Luke, who was living nearby in a shared flat with some friends and I met up with him in Camden in August 1993. We rekindled our relationship and saw each other for a few months when we could. Time spent with Luke was exciting but could be dark. I think I enjoyed the anticipation more than the actual time with him. Every friend of his seemed dodgy; every area we went to was run down and his dark lifestyle was so alien to mine, especially now that I had two young children.

I remember going along with Luke to a house on a run-down estate to visit his friends. As we walked into the front room, I had to stop myself from running out.

There was a baby crawling around the floor in a soiled nappy and there were overflowing ashtrays, empty beer cans and, worst of all, drug paraphernalia dotted around the entire room. When we left the house, thankfully after only fifteen minutes, we headed through the maze-like alleyways towards the station. Luke could sense my mood and asked if I was okay.

I hesitated, then said, 'No. I'm not. That place was horrendous. How could they let that baby crawl around in that filthy mess?'

Luke sighed. 'What do you expect? It's a safe house.'

Not having any idea what a safe house was, I asked Luke.

'It's where people avoiding the police hole up.'

I turned to Luke, open-mouthed.

'For God's sake! This is not the life I want!'

I was furious. But this was all my fault. It was never going to be chocolate and flowers with Luke, I knew that from the beginning. But this was the turning point for me.

I was fully aware that Luke was no good for me and I so wanted to make a go of it with Adam, despite our problems and differences. My main concern was a stable environment for the children, and their dad was the best option that I could choose.

I used Luke, not that he minded, but it was just a desperate attempt on my part to make Adam see the light, and it seemed to work. We had many heart-to-hearts while the children were asleep in bed, with Adam admitting that my fling with Luke had given him a taste of his own medicine. I cut off contact with Luke and, finally, Adam cut off all contact with Lesley. Luke accepted my decision well. It was never about love for Luke, it was just a bit of fun. And he was respectful of the fact that my children needed their father.

We patched things up and both made a huge effort, for the sake of the children. One of the positives of moving away from London was for a completely fresh start, minus both Lesley and Luke.

After a long search, we finally found our ideal home, within our budget, in Herefordshire. I was so excited to start again and to have our very own home but, looking back, I was naïve in thinking that everything would, or even could, be rosy.

Our major issue was centred around alcohol. When I found out I was pregnant, I gave up drinking, apart from the occasional white wine spritzer while socialising. But Adam's drinking increased, to the point where he was drinking every day.

I think back to our moving in day in August, Adam driving us in his beloved new Ford Focus, windows down, cool breeze wafting in, past the beautiful trees lining the pavements in our road. The cover of 'Perfect Day' an old Lou Reed song played on the car stereo, an apt song for our new start, if melancholic. I remember wishing that every day could feel like this.

The leaves were a riot of maroons, oranges and yellows, the blue sky accentuating the bright colours, the sun just starting to lose its summer punch. Adam pulled up to the house just behind the large white removals van, where two men were hoisting our worldly possessions to and from the neat little house.

'Here we are,' I said to the children, who were drowsy from the trip but beginning to reach their necks up to squint at their new home for the first time.

I remember glancing up at the dark window on the first-floor left side. That quarter of the house is overshadowed by the adjoining house which juts forward, so we can see right into the neighbour's downstairs hall via the window. The room on the left had already been allotted to Billy, as it is the smallest bedroom, and he is thirty minutes younger than his sister. He is too lively and distracted by boy's toys to notice anything untoward, but the room chills me.

The room has an empty feeling, almost a hollow feeling. It feels like it not only has no atmosphere, but that the life that should be in it is being sucked out of it. I can imagine feeling depressed in the room if I were to spend too much time in it. But Billy doesn't seem to notice anything. His happy spirit is unabated.

Maybe it is just my vivid imagination at play.

3

Moving in has been an exciting time, if nerve-wracking and tinged with sadness, as I am now an hour's drive away from family and friends.

Initially, settling in and decorating kept me busy, but it wasn't long before loneliness set in. I have had a chance to meet the new neighbours, who are mostly friendly, and have started to speak to some of the mothers at the school gates. But people in this area feel different somehow, more guarded and perhaps less worldly.

A couple of days after we moved in, feeling exhausted from shifting boxes and from all the emotional turmoil, I went out into the garden. I lay down on the long grass, flat on my back, and stared up at the beautiful sky dotted with small fluffy clouds. We have access to more sky now as the place is not so built up. A group of swallows flew past overhead, and I felt totally at peace.

We are now an hour from London, and we could be in a different country. The air is clean; the pace of life is much slower, and the crime rate is low. This is a nicer place to bring up the children, but I don't doubt that they will be desperate to escape once they reach their late teens. Our home town was within fifteen minutes' drive of the hustle and bustle of central London. This area, in comparison, is more about tea and cake and reading groups.

Most people do seem nice, but most seem to be missing that wit and edge I am used to. Finding work locally hasn't been particularly easy but I have now managed to find some admin work at a local doctor's surgery for three days a week while the children are at school. It doesn't pay particularly well but it will do for the short term.

I work on the top floor of a very old, listed building, along with two other women. The upper floors are said to have a ghost in residence but in all honesty, I have never felt anything, yet. But that doesn't surprise me, because my workmates and I are incessantly talking from the time I turn up until I leave to go to pick the children up from school. I don't doubt that it would be a different story if I was alone there in silence.

However, our house does feel a little odd, as if you are never quite alone, but not in a comfortable way. Prior to moving in, Adam and I had spent a couple of weekends in a row, minus the children, carrying out some deep cleaning and basic decorating to ensure the children could go straight into their bedrooms when we moved in. This time together was quite nice; we chatted and laughed at times, both working towards a common aim and mucking in together.

One of the nicer days during that time was when we carried our huge wardrobe up the stairs. Adam would usually be tense when moving furniture or carrying out DIY, but this day was different. Adam went first, walking backwards up the stairs, supporting the base of the wardrobe whilst I walked forwards, supporting the base. We were silent for a few moments as we lifted the extremely heavy object. Then I said, 'I don't even like this wardrobe.'

Adam began to laugh, and I joined him. We ended up weak with laughter, me kneeling on the stairs with one knee, Adam sitting on a stair near the top, barely able to keep hold of the monstrously heavy object between us. When we finally got the unloved object into our bedroom, we had a break by switching on Adam's stereo and finding a lively radio station, sitting on the floor and smoking. I can't remember what we spoke about, but we had a bonding moment.

But I don't kid myself that things are going to improve. Our arguments continue. Arguments about money, arguments about décor, arguments about nothing.

During our decorating weekends, we also started to paint the open-plan front room/dining room. My plans are to have this room zen-like, with minimal clutter and neutral colours. However, having two young children may not allow this, as they seem to spread their belongings over the entire house.

This is the first time that I have lived in a house with an open-plan area, and it will take some getting used to. We call it the front room out of habit, but technically it is the front and back room. It means that Adam and I are forced to spend every evening in the same room together, which is not ideal. But it can be converted in time if need be.

The garden is a real bonus. One hundred foot long, with two ponds, one at the front and one at the rear. There's no doubt that loads of work needs to be done to get the garden up to scratch, but it is a great blank canvas, with a stone shed, a lawn stretching three quarters of the way down the garden and a variety of shrubs and trees to discover. I know next to nothing about gardens, but my mum and dad are keen gardeners, so they have promised to help me plan the garden makeover when I am ready.

We painted Darcy's room in a DIY pink-and-lilac sponge print and placed a huge pink neon light on the wall. Darcy's room feels exactly right, light, airy and, well, stable. Unlike her brother's room, it doesn't give off a negative vibe.

To perk Billy's new room up, we spent hours scraping off the awful anaglypta wallpaper with sponges, water and a scraper, painting the walls a bright sky blue, then scrunching up a sponge and adding white marble-like touches to look like clouds. I then attached individual glow-in-the-dark stars to the ceiling, which give off a green glow when it gets dark.

But despite the coat of paint, Billy's room just feels off. I asked a neighbour, who seems to know everyone's business, whether the former owner, an elderly man, had died in the house and she replied that yes, they had found him in the front bedroom on the left. I remember smiling at her specific detail. It doesn't surprise me that someone died here, it just goes some way to explaining the gloomy atmosphere. It's not just the room, though. The house in general feels wrong.

I think back to our little flat where we had lived before and it also had its share of spooky goings-on, but generally there was a happy feeling about the place. And when I think of my childhood home, with its haunted feel and spooky history, it also felt much happier than this place.

Could my own feelings of doubt and unhappiness be contributing to the gloomy atmosphere of this house? It's highly possible.

In addition to any potential ghosts, I don't doubt that the ghost of my relationship with Adam is also a factor.

4

Late afternoon, still light outside, I notice that Billy has a high temperature and very pink cheeks, so I give him some Calpol and snuggle up with him on his bed, placing a cold wet flannel on his forehead to bring his temperature down further. He plays on his Gameboy for a little while, but I gently take it away from him, encouraging him to rest his eyes. He falls asleep quickly.

Darcy pads in as quiet as a mouse, with her new Harry Potter book, *The Chamber of Secrets*.

'Shh,' I say, smiling and putting my finger to my lips, making room for Darcy on the bed, her legs tangling with mine. I quietly read a chapter to her, ensuring I do all the voices as she likes me to. Occasionally I forget, but occasionally on purpose, I do a deep voice for Hermione and a high voice for Hagrid, which makes her giggle. I love reading these books to Darcy, who is a real bookworm, and I think I enjoy them as much as she does. She snuggles down and, with the quiet combined with the heat radiating from Billy, I start to drift off myself.

I am nearly asleep when I hear firm footsteps walk across the uncarpeted wooden floor, from my bedroom opposite the hall right up to the bed by my side. There is no one else in the house. The children are both sound asleep on the bed with me. I don't open my eyes immediately as I am too drowsy, and I know who it is. I think, with a flash of anger, *Get away from my children*. I open my eyes and, as expected, there is no one there. I have become so used to him, I drift off to sleep without much concern.

Here is the boy in the electric chair again. He is crying and begging me to help him. This poor boy, he is going to die in that chair and there is nothing I can do to help. Even though I am standing directly in front of him, I know in my heart that any attempts to free him would be futile. All I can do is comfort him. I lay my hand on his little hand, my face awash with tears, and tell him 'It's okay. I'm here with you.'

I wake up, alarmed and think someone has died. No sooner have I thought this, the home telephone starts to ring and is answered by Adam. I can hear his deep muffled voice talking to the caller. It is now dark outside, and the green stars glow on the ceiling of Billy's room. I move my sleeping children's arms and legs gently away from me and creep out of the bedroom so as not to wake them.

Slowly descending the stairs, I see Adam standing in the downstairs hallway looking up at me.

'Your sister called. Can you call her back?' he says, then wanders off into the front room. I call Alice, heart racing and when she picks up, I blurt. 'Has someone died?'

Silence on the other end and then, 'How did you know?'

My heart thumps but I can't easily explain so I don't try.

'Oh my God, who?', thinking my children are here with me safe, thank God.

'Luke,' she replies. I sit down on the bottom stair and she goes on to explain that he had been in prison for armed robbery, and he had been found hanging by the prison guards. I ask when.

'Last night,' she replies.

My dreams, I realise, are of Luke, who was symbolised by the little boy with the jet-black hair and blue eyes. Although the details are vague, I know they are signs. I have always thought of Luke as a lost little boy, and that is perhaps why I dreamt of him in this way, as I know that he had gone down the wrong path and was a criminal. The electric chair was clearly connected in my mind with him being in prison, so potentially the prison system killed him as he committed suicide.

I haven't seen or heard from Luke for about five years, but he has always been on my mind. Sadly, his untimely death was inevitable and no real surprise, due to his chaotic lifestyle, but I still feel deeply saddened and I mentally send him love, wherever he may be.

I go into the front room to tell Adam the sad news. As I walk in, I see that Adam is sitting at the dining table, smoking a roll-up and playing his music. I feel a wave of pity for him. He strikes me as a boy who doesn't want to grow up.

Adam is surprised, as I tell him that Luke has died, and as he always is when someone of our age dies suddenly.

'Whoah! How did he die?'

'He committed suicide, apparently,' I replied.

'Really?' Adam rubs his hands on his forehead. 'That's awful.'

'I know. Luke was mixed up, but I didn't expect him to do that.'

'Whoah!,' Adam says again, trying to process the news.

And I dreamt about it before it happened. I don't say this out loud, as Adam would be dismissive at best, downright mean at worst.

5

That evening, I sit in front of the TV as I can't sleep. I am watching, but not concentrating on, *Shooting Stars* starring my favourite comedians Vic Reeves and Bob Mortimer. The comedy duo never fail to make me laugh, with their silly antics, but I just can't stop thinking of Luke's death and my dreams.

The poor boy in the dreams was Luke, of that I'm sure. But what did the rest of the dream mean? And what about the steps up to Billy's bed when I was lying with the children? Had my visitor been jealous that I was not in my own bed? Had I foreseen Luke's death? Or did I somehow psychically connect with him?

The curtains are open despite the darkness outside, a tree silhouetted against the darkest blue sky, and I pull the curtains closed and try to come to some sort of a conclusion. As I settle back into the sofa, I glance up at the light bulb in the centre of the ceiling for no reason.

Suddenly, there is a bright flash of light, a smashing sound and the smell of burning I leap off the sofa when the light bulb not only blows, but seems to throw itself violently across the room, smashing on the uncarpeted floorboards. My heart hammering, I try to calm myself down and think logically. When had I put that bulb in, was it perhaps taken from an old light fitting and was on its way out? No, this was a new bulb that I had bought particularly for this light fitting as it was a warm white for a softer glow. Or it was, before it decided to smash.

I had read somewhere that the spirit world tries to communicate through electricity or water. I really have just about had enough of all these spooky events. I haven't got the time or the energy. It could be that the wattage of the bulb was perhaps too powerful for the fitting. But to fly across the room like that? It is then that the lightbulb smashing exercise from my recent dream comes to me. I was smashing lightbulbs because they were lit up and there was water nearby. But that doesn't correlate with what just happened.

The visitor follows me from home to home, so he clearly isn't connected with my childhood home, as I once thought. When I think back to the ages I have been when the visits have occurred, it becomes evident that there is a seven-year connection. Age seven, age fourteen, age twenty-one and now age twenty-eight. Will he come back at age thirty-five? I feel that I will be dead of exhaustion by then. I barely think of him in the years between visits. I don't think I forget him totally, but he is put back into the recesses of my mind. And now he is centre stage, again. I clear up the smashed bulb and get back to trying to watch my programme. I am becoming almost blasé when unexplained otherworldly events occur now.

Then, from upstairs, a piercing scream, I leap up. Oh no, who is that? Which child? … Darcy. I race up to her bedroom, taking three stairs at a time.

'Okay, it's okay, Mummy's here!' Heart thudding, I find her standing beside her bed with a look of terror on her face.

'Mummy, a man—' dear God, no!

'It's just a bad dream, honey.' I crouch down and take her in my arms. Her hot little body is shivering and, sure enough, when I feel her forehead, she now also seems to have a temperature. I pick her up and hold her close, taking her in to my bed. Adam sits up sleepily, late to the party as always, and comforts her while I go down to get the Calpol and spoon.

Back in the room with Darcy, I give her the medicine and I think that the temperature must have caused the hallucinations. I can't bear to think that she is suffering with the visits like I do. She is seven years old! Forget that, enough. For self-preservation, I have learnt how to blank something completely out of my head if it is too much for me to bear. I kind of push it backwards in my brain and it sits in a section that will one day need no doubt explode out.

I sit on the side of the bed, facing Darcy.

'Honey, when you're not well and you get a high temperature, it can make you feel really hot, and high temperatures can make you have bad dreams and hallucinations.'

Darcy says, 'It was only a bad dream,' and she touches my heart as she nods, convincing herself of this.

'Daddy,' I say to Adam, as I have been using that name for him in front of the children as Darcy sometimes calls him Adam, which he can't stand. 'Can Darcy sleep in here tonight?'

'Of course,' Adam replies. 'I'll put A DVD on to settle you down, Darcy.'

Adam puts one of her new films, *Jumanji*, on the little portable DVD player and Darcy snuggles down on my side of the bed, falling asleep before the film begins.

I decide to sleep downstairs on the sofa. I'm exhausted and don't want any more dreams, visitations or nasty surprises, so I pop a couple of strong sleeping pills, swig a bit of whiskey which Adam has left on the coffee table and settle down to sleep.

6

In the morning, sitting on my bed, stroking Darcy's hair, I know that she has inevitably caught the infection that Billy has. Just recently, they seem to pick up never-ending germs. Swaddled up in a cosy blanket, her temperature has gone down further as she is sucking on an ice-lolly to cool her. She is watching *The Worst Witch* on DVD, one of her favourite programmes, and looking so poorly that I decide not to broach the subject of nightmares for now. I check on Billy and then head downstairs to get some fresh water and Calpol for the children.

Adam has gone off to work and left his mobile phone on the dining table, along with a pile of loose change and some receipts. I'm tempted to have a look through his phone to see if he is still in contact with Lesley. I shouldn't, I think. I start to busy myself with making sure the children are settled and their temperatures have been brought down, then tidying the kitchen and pottering around.

And then, without much of a thought process, I abruptly throw down the dishcloth and come back to the phone. There is one unread text message on his mobile.

From Lesley. 'I'll call you tomorrow after 9 x'.

After nine, he would be at work, or certainly out of the house. And the 'x' clearly means a kiss. So, he is cheating again. Or, at the very least, going behind my back by being in contact with her. I can't even phone him to have it out as his mobile is right here.

For the rest of the day, the message consumes me. I try to distract myself by calling Layla for a catch-up. I tell myself that I won't mention the message from Lesley, as Layla hates Adam enough as it is, but of course I do.

'Oh no! Zoe, please don't put up with this any more. He's had way too many chances!' Layla is furious.

'Or, I could play him at his own game?' I reply, childishly.

'Don't lower yourself, get rid.'

Layla is my go-to person for matters of the heart. And although she is straight down the line and no-nonsense with her advice, she has never liked Adam so she wouldn't ever attempt to put his side across or defend his actions. But no one can defend the indefensible.

Layla has a relatively unusual relationship with her partner, Si, at least compared to anyone else I know. Although they have a very close bond, they live separately and always have. But it works for them and over time I have seen that the positives far outweigh the negatives. I clearly remember a conversation on the subject with a colleague of mine whom I had introduced to Layla on a night out. Lisa, the previous receptionist of the recruitment agency where I worked, had asked Layla what felt like ten thousand questions about the set up. She was embarrassing me by overreacting to what she seemed to see as some type of social scandal.

At one point, Lisa had asked, 'Aren't you worried that as he doesn't live with you, he will find it easier to be unfaithful?'

'No, Lisa,' Layla replied. 'Anyone can be unfaithful if that is the way they are.' Layla had given me a look that said a thousand words, and I had blushed furiously.

As the children seemed too poorly to go out, I had arranged for a doctor from the surgery to do a home visit to see the children. Typically, they had perked up a fair bit when the doctor arrived, and I felt guilty that I had taken up his valuable time. But he confirmed that they both had sore throats and Billy required antibiotics for a throat infection.

I am pleased that the doctor who attended wasn't my actual doctor, who is also my boss at the surgery. He is quite aloof, and I would have felt uncomfortable with him seeing my humble home, not to mention me with my dressing gown still on in the afternoon and a thick gloopy green face mask just beginning to set and crack on my face.

When Adam comes in from work, he can immediately tell that something is up. I find it difficult to wait until the children have gone to sleep for the night, but I somehow manage to.

I don't admit to having looked at his mobile phone, but he will realise how I have found out eventually, as he will be able to see that the text message has been read.

'So, what's going on with Lesley?' I sit across from him at the dining table, looking directly into his eyes. He doesn't answer immediately and averts his eyes as he rubs his forehead. He pauses for too long, starts to speak and I raise my hand and say, 'No, that's fine, your face says it all.' And the conversation ends there. I don't want to know the details. That way, there is less to go into the secure box at the back of my brain.

I had known all along if I am completely truthful with myself. I thought that maybe moving away we could make a fresh start but even if he hadn't been unfaithful, and Lesley didn't exist, our relationship wasn't strong enough to even want to hold on to. There is a part of me that is glad that it is Adam who is causing the ultimate break-down of our relationship. At least I will always have that.

I go up to bed, checking in on the children quickly, just to look at people that I love. I feel upset, but I also feel another emotion that is more difficult to pinpoint, and I realise it is relief. This is the death knell for our relationship. I don't believe that I will ever regain my trust for Adam, but for now, I will try my best to keep things amicable.

7

Early evening, I start to get ready for my night out. I was supposed to be going to the cinema to see *Armageddon* with Adam for a rare night out, and our neighbour was going to babysit, but under the circumstances, I am relieved that I am going alone and getting out of the house for a few hours.

This will be the first time that I've ever been to the cinema on my own and I'm a little nervous. I put on my cargo trousers with a blue tie-dyed vest and clip my hair up in a messy bun. I don't tell Adam where I am going, as he would have forgotten that we had made plans anyway, I just tell him that I am going out. I sit at the table with him, without speaking, for a few minutes prior to heading off, silently hoping he will ask me where I am going, and I could reply 'That's none of your business.' How pathetic, I think. He wouldn't care anyway. I grab a raincoat on the way out, as it has started to rain quite heavily.

I pull up in a small car park behind a bar near to the cinema, in the dark. In the near empty car park, there is just a workman's van and a small beaten-up Ford Escort. The rain must have kept most people away. As

I lock the car and head to my destination, I accidentally step into a huge puddle which has collected in a dip in the bumpy tarmac. Ah, shit, I think, as I feel the water seeping up the bottom of my trousers. I side-step and then glance down at the huge puddle angrily. Neon lights from the rear of the bar are reflected in the water.

As I see my reflection in the puddle, I see a dark mass next to my left shoulder. It looks like it's moving around, like dark smoke. I look to my left and see nothing. What the hell was that? As I think this, my phone buzzes in my bag. I had set an alarm so as not to be late for the cinema, so I hurry off, with wet shoes, thinking I should have stayed in.

As it turns out, despite the bad start, the whole cinema experience is lovely. I forget about my wet feet after a short while, as the interior of the cinema is a real surprise, decked out in an art deco style.

Even the young staff are dressed smartly to match the décor, both boys and girls in black waistcoats neatly done up, with white long-sleeved shirts underneath. I get myself some popcorn and a bright blue Slush Puppie which, to my mind, is part of the experience, and walk in to Screen One.

As I settle in to enjoy the film, I look around at the décor. Decked out in maroon and cream, the ceiling light is magnificent, a huge showy chandelier in true art deco style with huge diamond shaped glass droplets, surrounded by layers of upturned triangular cream- and beige-coloured glass. The wall uplighters are more compact but in the same style.

I zone out of the adverts and trailers and think of the dark mass that I saw in my reflection. I feel like I have experienced that before, but I can't think when. Am I possessed? There have been so many weird occurrences over the year. Layla's mum's comment to me in the pub when I was younger springs to mind. This has always stayed with me. Could it be a case of self-fulfilling prophecy, caused by Deana's idiotic comment? No, it runs deeper than that and goes much further.

The film is enjoyable if a bit too long at two and a half hours. I had finished my popcorn before the trailers had even finished. I also felt like I needed a chiropractor after sitting in one spot for that long. I think of Layla as she would love this cinema. I must contact her soon and invite her over, but the film we watch would be problematic, as she prefers a romantic film whereas I like darker films such as horrors, thrillers and disaster films.

Whilst watching a film, I always get fully immersed and put myself in the shoes of the protagonists and I think, what would I do in that situation? It's as if I'm preparing myself for every eventuality. The vivid imagination comment made all those years ago by the doctor comes back to me. There's no doubt that this is true of me. But that doesn't explain how can I see some things before they happen? This makes me think that this was perhaps how I was aware of Adam's affair with Lesley all along. Not just through Adam's cold behaviour towards me but through signs in my dreams.

I need to keep searching for the answers.

Maybe it really is my dreams that hold the answers to all the 7s?

1997

1996

1995

1994

1993

1992

PART FIVE
21 YEARS OLD

1991 – 28 years ago
1

I am invisible and, in front of me, there is a woman, and it is me, walking towards work using the short cut next to Our Price. The woman is holding hands with a girl to her left and a boy to her right. The children are aged around five or six years old. Even though I am observing them from behind so that I can only see the back of all three of them, I have a sense that they all seem happy and content, and in no rush. The little girl looks up at the woman and says something and the woman smiles and replies, but I can't hear what is being said. The two little ones feel like they could be my children, but I'm a long way off from having children yet.

Then I find myself back at my old home, with various family members dotted around: Mum and Dad, Uncle Pete, Grandad.

I am standing in the hallway at the bottom of the stairs, and I don't want to go upstairs, but for some reason I must. Because of the children? Are they my children?

I must do this, but I know there is something dark and evil up there. A ghost? Then I see ghosts coming from upstairs, one at a time, sweeping through the air towards my face and trying to scare me, but I have an anger building inside of me, so I gather all my rage and roar at them. This seems to be working, as the ghosts disappear each time I roar. I must be brave, and although I'm afraid, I cannot show it. I know that if I show the ghosts no fear, I have the feeling they will stop bothering me. And I know that I now must go up the stairs, on my own.

Although I am still frightened, I walk up the stairs faster than I want to and, perhaps because I am being bold, nothing bothers me on the way up. Relieved, but cautious, I go into the first room I come to, the bathroom at the top of the stairs on the right. The décor looks dreary and old-fashioned as it is decorated in the avocado colour, with green jungle-looking wallpaper, from when I was little. Mum and Dad have a modern bathroom now, so I must have somehow gone back in time.

Before I reach the bath, I know what I'm going to see. I look down and see that it is full of water, but the water is a thick dark red. The bath is full of blood. There are a pair of pale white severed hands floating in the bath. I can see that the hands once belonged to an adult male as they are large and man-like. Hovering above the bath is a dark grey smoky substance, swirling around like a tempestuous storm cloud. It gives me a feeling of pure dread. It is so wrong.

I then look behind me and Bob is coming in through the bathroom door... I feel like my mind is going to break, I am so terrified. I'm stuck in between two horrors, and I start to back towards the blood-filled bath... It's only water... It's only coloured water...

My eyes flicker open. My heart is hammering, but I feel the terror dissipating. I'm confused and keep reminding myself that it was a dream. But Bob was just about to get me, I find him so terrifying. Bob is not real, he's just a character in *Twin Peaks*, I know that, but it felt horribly real. I try to think of the actor who plays Bob to try to minimise my fear of the character.

Those ghosts flying down the stairs, the evil feeling coming from upstairs. That had to be my worst dream for a while. I feel like it means something. What is my subconscious trying to tell me?

I must remember to ask Mum if I had any type of bad scare in the bathroom or on the stairs when I was young. Mind you, all those years of sleepwalking, I suppose it could be anything. I look over at my alarm clock and the bright red digits read 02.50. I really need to get some sleep as I've got Anna's funeral tomorrow.

I am trying my best to drift off fully again and change the dream to suit me, then... there's something in the room with me. It's awful, it feels evil. I can't see it, but I know it's there. I try to call out, but no sound comes. Am I still dreaming? I try to look around, but my head won't move, so I just dart my eyes about. The alarm clock says now says 03.04 a.m. and the display is flashing. I hate this feeling of impending doom. I can't move at all. Then a loud noise starts buzzing in my ears and when I shut my eyes, I can see black-and-white flashes, like electricity. It feels like the black-and-white fuzz when you are looking for a TV channel.

I know it's not Bob here with me; he's a fictional character. This must be Jacob again from when I was young. No, I must not give him a name, it makes him feel like a friend. How did I not realise that it was him straight away? It's been a long time. How long? I'm panicking now. I squeeze my eyes shut and then I realise that my feet are icy cold. I glance down and see that the covers have been pulled back. Please, no. Not again.

2

Standing in the grounds of the church, I look up at the winter sky, a stark bright white, set against black-looking trees. Not a hint of green, but glimpses of orange autumn leaves clinging on to branches despite the odds. I glance over at the gravestones, where once beautiful wreaths lie in varying degrees of life, adorning loved ones' plots.

Waiting for Anna's funeral to begin, I stand with a group of friends and acquaintances, trying to hold myself together. Vestiges of last night's dream and then the visit from... *the visitor*. I refuse to give him a name, I think. Don't think about that now. Think of Anna.

I am dreading this, and it doesn't help that I can't shake off last night's visit. It stands to reason that I would have nightmares prior to the funeral as my mind needs to process this, but the dream felt like it meant something. Like my dreams are trying to send me signs.

Anna's death has been a real shock to the system, the first time in my life that I have experienced the death of someone of my age and the first time I have been really affected by death. I was too young and self-involved to understand the loss of elderly family members in the past.

Anna had just passed her driving test, two weeks before the crash. She had been desperate to pass her test and I knew what it meant to her to pass first time.

On the morning of the accident, she had been driving to work, a temp job for a huge local company, and she somehow clipped a curb, the car flipped over, and she suffered whiplash and irreversible brain damage. The life support machine was turned off after two days, her heartbroken mum left bereft.

She had been a close school friend; we got up to a lot of mischief together. I hadn't liked her initially; I had thought she weas childish and a bit mean, but once we started to spend some time together, she became my best friend at school. She was very cheeky and naughty, not liked by everyone, but I knew the real person and she had a heart of gold. But as time went on, we got up to more and more mischief and my mum hadn't wanted me to mix with her, which was understandable, I suppose, as we were naughty when we were together.

I think back to some of our crazy adventures. We had been massive attention seekers when together. We once hid in her loft to pretend we had been kidnapped, but we only lasted about two hours and Anna somehow managed to fall out of the loft. Another time, we ramped things up and ran off to the park at night and hid in a children's wooden playhouse for the night. Our parents and extended family members, along with the police, hunted for us through the night and when we emerged the following day, we pretended we had got tired and fallen asleep whilst out.

I am so sad that we had lost touch in recent years, due to work and boyfriends and just life moving on. And

I regret that I didn't go to visit her in the hospital while she was on life support. I don't really understand, myself, why I didn't. I think I was too scared; I just couldn't face it. If I could turn back time and see her one last time, I would.

Inside the church, which is packed to the rafters, I glance at Anna's mum, who is understandably distraught. I inhale and exhale slowly, trying to gather myself. This is going to be tough. The wording, read out by Anna's older sister who holds it together amazingly, is beautiful and really highlights the cheeky character that Anna was. The entire funeral party, including myself, flip from laughing to crying and back again in the space of seconds.

When the huge velvet curtains start to close, and Anna's coffin starts to disappear, to the sounds of 'Somewhere out there' by James Ingram and Linda Ronstadt, I can feel my emotions rising, overwhelming me. It's so final, somehow. She has been gone for two weeks but closing the curtains is like putting a full stop on her life. I feel like running out of the church, but then my inner voice says pay your respects, which calms me and allows me to get myself together. When the service has finished, it is a sweet relief to get out into the bright white glare of the sky.

Although I have thought about her constantly, I haven't dreamt of Anna since she died, but I know I will dream of her in time. When loved ones die, I seem to dream of them a few months after their death and they never speak in my dreams, they are just with me, standing next to me, giving off a feeling of protection.

A fresh chill in the January air with a biting wind, muted voices respectful of the dead. Now that the funeral has finished, we walk slowly away from the church in small groups, some comforting others, some lost in their own thoughts. I feel a sense of contentment that the funeral has been such a beautiful celebration of Anna's life and a sense of relief that this is now over, and we have now laid Anna to rest.

Welcoming the cold, biting air as I emerge from the church, I start to walk alone towards the car park and spot a friend, Becky, ahead. She turns and waits for me to catch up.

'Hey, are you okay?'

'Yes.' I nod and smile.

'That was a really lovely service,' she says.

'It was,' I reply. I have nothing to compare it to, but it felt fitting.

A man I don't recognise joins us.

'Zoe, this is Adam.'

I meet his eyes and it feels too personal, a shock to the system. I feel an instant attraction, his gorgeous hazel eyes, nice smile and full lips. I have read that it is commonplace for funeral attendees to feel in the mood for sex to somehow balance the feelings of morbidity associated with death, in order to reaffirm life.

I can confirm that this is true.

3

Things have progressed extremely fast with Adam. The last couple of days have been exciting. We have talked on the phone for hours and hours, into the night, and I feel like I have known him for a long time. There's no awkwardness between us, just a real chemistry that we both feel and can't deny. And he is so comical, with a dry wit and sarcasm that I love. Where some of my friends concentrate on looks alone, I favour the cheeky bad boys. The classically good-looking boys do absolutely nothing for me.

Just three days after meeting, we lie together on a huge beach blanket on my bedroom floor, having decided my single bed isn't big enough for our impromptu indoor picnic. My mum and dad have gone away for the weekend, so we are playing house. We went off to Sainsbury's together this afternoon, like an old married couple, and bought pita bread, olives, taramasalata, houmous, beer and wine and we are enjoying our indoor picnic and watching a video. We both really love watching films, and as I don't have a video player, Adam headed off to buy a cheap second-hand player from a guy who had advertised in the local paper. When Adam turned up with it, I was so touched. As he set it up to work with my little TV, he became even more attractive to me. I am so easily pleased, I think.

'So, what do you want to watch first?' he asked, taking a pile of VHS tapes out of a plastic Sainsbury's bag. He had rented *Parenthood*; *Black Rain*, a thriller starring Andy Garcia; *Flatliners*, a horror starring Kiefer Sutherland, and *Pretty Woman*. I was particularly touched that he chose *Parenthood*, as it stars Keanu Reeves. Adam is not keen on him, calling his acting 'wooden' but I told him, in one of our marathon phone conversations, that I have liked Keanu ever since I saw him in an old film, *River's Edge*. *Pretty Woman*, however, was clearly for Adam's benefit, as he likes Julia Roberts.

I would say that we watched all the films, but we watched very little of them. We were too busy chatting, laughing and getting intimate.

At one point, I noticed there was something left in the plastic bag, so I opened the bag to have a peek and pulled out a child's cheap and chunky plastic crown, breast plate and sword.

'What the…?' I ask.

He laughs. 'This is my nephew's. I just stuffed the videos in a bag and didn't check what was in there.'

I persuade him to get dressed up in the kiddies dress-up knight's kit and, with the camera shaking due to my laughter, I manage to take some snaps of him posing with a silly grin on his face.

Adam heads off at around ten p.m., as he has work in the morning and is being picked up at stupid o'clock outside his house.

That night, I dream of Adam and I dancing about happily in some waste ground, acting the fool. At one point Adam lifts my arms up and twirls me around, and when I face him again, his face has transformed to something evil, with a bone-chilling smile and red eyes.

In the morning, despite my nightmares, all I want to do is to be with Adam. Work seems to drag to eternity, and I can't concentrate at all.

Then, finally, at five p.m., I reapply my make-up in the pokey mirror in the bathroom at work. I am so excited to see him again. It has only been a day, but I am well and truly hooked. Armed with an overnight bag, I arrive at Adam's house in a cab. His maisonette is on a horrible grey high-rise estate and the house itself is dark and gloomy. We were always told to steer clear of this estate when we were growing up, and we did, for the most part. But here I am.

When he opens the front door, we grin at each other and can't stop grinning every time we catch each other's eyes. It's so nice to feel this way. His mum is shut away in her bedroom, so I don't get to meet her.

Up in Adam's bedroom, I hand him his gift that I had bought at Woolworths during my lunch hour. I had bought him a CD player along with three CDs, a selection of Bob Marley & The Wailers, U2 and Simple Minds. The Bob Marley CD is more for my benefit and the other two are his musical taste, although I do like some of the songs.

As Adam is setting up the CD player, he tests the radio stations by finding a station that sounds good and he then jiggles the antenna about, every which way. 'Dizzy' by Vic Reeves and the Wonder Stuff comes on, and we start to dance around like lunatics. Adam's over-accentuated moves, especially his crazy attempt at hip thrusting, are so funny, I crack up laughing. As so often happens, whilst enjoying myself, I am reminded of some awful elements of the previous night's dream, but I push the negativity aside.

Later, we lie together in his bed, listening to the CDs on a loop and chatting. Needing a change, I flick the switch for the radio, and Enigma's 'Sadeness Part 1' plays, which is a lovely mellow song and exactly right for this late in the evening.

In the dark, we lie facing each other and I chat away happily but quietly, so as not to wake his mum. I can just barely see his face, and suddenly, his features look evil, evil eyes matching an evil smile, and I push myself backwards in fright.

Adam quickly leans over and switches the lamp on. And then, to my horror, he turns over to face me.

'What the hell…' I am totally terrified.

'What's wrong?' he says, and I have clearly frightened him too.

'I was looking at your face and it kind of turned evil... but then you turned over and it was actually the back of your head I was looking at...'

'For fuck's sake,' he says, sitting up in bed. 'You scared the shit out of me!' My heart is beating way too fast, and I try to justify what I think I saw.

After going back and forth with Adam, who is upset that I had thought he was 'evil', if only for a second, I decide that a mixture of Anna's death and funeral and the recent nighttime visits and nightmares have given me the jitters. It is no more than that. Adam goes off on a tangent about me thinking he has 'two faces' and teases me in a half-joking way.

After the scare, I try to get some sleep. The more time we spend together, the more I like Adam but the more I know that he is completely unsuitable for me and I for him, but I don't care. Love has head reared its head and I am hooked. But is it love or just sexual chemistry? He is undemonstrative, black and white to the extreme and, apart from us both enjoying films and music and having a laugh together, we share no common interests. But the chemistry is undoubtedly there. My last thought, just before I fall asleep, is something Adam had said earlier.

Is he two-faced? I think. A strange thought that I shake off, and then sleep comes.

4

Despite quite a few reservations, it has been a whirlwind
month and we have now moved into a rented apartment
together. My mum and dad are furious, as they think I
hardly know Adam, but I feel that I do. For a while now
I have been looking to leave home and be more
independent. By a happy coincidence, Adam was
having to leave home himself as his mum was
downsizing, so I took the leap and jumped in with him.
But I do have it in the back of my mind, like a safety
blanket, that if it doesn't work out between us, I can
always go home.

It is now mid-February and our poky little flat
above a Robert Dyas shop is freezing cold. The heavy
snow and freezing conditions don't seem to be letting
up, and the inside of the horrible, chipped wood-framed
windows in the front room have a thin layer of ice which
I continually must wipe. It doesn't help that the flat is
situated on a corner and there's nothing to stop the cold
wind hitting one side of the building. The flat is also tiny
and is better suited to one person. We have managed to
borrow a couple of little electric heaters from a friend.
They blast out a ferocious heat, but they are very heavy

on the electricity meter, so we limit the time we have them on. Well, Adam does. When he is out, I have them on full blast for the entire time.

On the plus side, the flat is relatively cheap to rent, and it is situated in the high street, near to my work, and in the centre of all the high street shops, pubs and restaurants. We can only afford to eat out at Wimpy, but that's fine for now.

When we are together in the evenings, we spend most of our time lying in bed, watching films, me smoking cigarettes, Adam smoking joints. I don't mind Adam smoking cannabis, but I don't get on with it myself. It just makes me feel queasy and a bit paranoid.

I remember smoking my first ever joint when I was around thirteen years old, with Anna and an older guy, whose name escapes me. It was lovely summer's day, and we were in the park. The effects of the joint and the older guy – who the hell was he? Had we just met him walking along? – doing action-man style poses, stiff arms bent at the elbow, knees bent, to make us laugh. The combination did the trick and we laughed until we cried. But it was never the same after that and I stopped bothering with it.

Adam can be very funny at times, but he is the least romantic person I have ever met and is quite often downright rude. There is a rough edge to him, and I wonder whether it's because he hasn't grown up with sisters. He doesn't seem to see the difference between male and female feelings, to the point where he can say quite hurtful things. I had mentioned my dreams to him recently and said that I thought sometimes things I dreamt of came true and he accused me of talking shit. I'm not used to being spoken to in that way, so we had yet another argument.

The night before last I dreamt of Anna for the first time since her death. I haven't written the dream down, so I can only remember snippets. I know we were in a supermarket and there was an alien invasion of some sort, and we were loading up with goods for survival. We only had one basket, so we loaded up on biscuits. Then Anna walked to my old home with me, and we said goodbye. My heart ached as I knew she had to go for now. I wanted to say to her 'I live with Adam now, not here!' but she had gone, and I felt like she was telling me to go home. She had been by my side and supporting me. It was a nice dream and I had woken up with a sense of contentment.

Unfortunately, my nightmares have come back with a vengeance, and last night's horror involved me laying in a bed and a room that I didn't recognise, and the room slowly shrank down, smaller and smaller, until I was lying in a room the size of a funeral casket.

Then, at some point during the dream, I heard a piercing siren noise, and I woke up, realising straight away that the smoke alarm was going off. I raced out to the hallway and found that there was no smoke. Relieved, I pressed the off button.

I drifted off to sleep again and, annoyingly close to sleep, the alarm went off again. Adam was sleeping right through all of this, which annoyed me even more. I leapt up again, and yet again there was no smoke. I grabbed a chair, climbed up and took out the battery. I had once heard that faulty batteries could trigger the alarm. I found a spare battery, still in its packaging, in the messy drawer in the kitchen and replaced the battery.

Back to bed. I woke again to the alarm screeching but this time I woke from a nice dream involving Anna and I made no pretence in being quiet this time, shouting, 'For fuck's sake!' Before I crashed out into the hall and ripped the battery out, I noticed that the alarm display said 02.05 a.m. That time rings a bell for some reason. I think to myself if the fire alarm goes off again without a battery, what then?

My nightmares have ramped up recently and the interrupted sleep is causing me problems at work, due to the lack of concentration. I'm not too bothered though, as there is another job that I am thinking of applying for if I do get the sack. But aside from my mostly horrible dreams, I am having fun at playing house and feeling grown-up. Everything is kind of okay.

And then I had the BT phone line installed. And then Lesley started to phone.

Adam had been seeing Lesley for the last couple of years until they split up last year, well before we met. I had grilled Adam about the ins and outs of their relationship, wanting to know absolutely everything. He didn't give much. But to his credit, he didn't slag her off to me and just kept his cards close to his chest. This makes me think he will be the same when we inevitably split up. I certainly hope so.

The first time she phoned, last week, I was supposed to be at work but had called in sick because, frankly, it was too cold to get out of bed. When I finally crept out of bed mid-morning, I pulled on some woolly socks and a thick jumper and crept over to the heater to get some much-needed heat circulating around. Then the phone rang. I answered and there was silence on the other end. I didn't think much of it.

Then it rang again. Silence again. There was no way to find out who had called. Lesley popped into my mind. I wonder whether Adam has her phone number in with his papers. I know he doesn't have a telephone book, that's way too organised. I open the drawer which has been allocated to Adam's birth certificate, passport, cheque book and his general rubbish. I can't find anything that relates to phone numbers, and then come across a battered old leather diary and have a flick through. At the back of the diary, is a section for telephone numbers which he had, by some miracle, filled in. Sure enough, Lesley's number is in the list.

As I dial the number, I think Lesley must have known it was me trying to reach her. No 'hello'. Just a few seconds of silence and then, 'Who is this?' More silence.

'I'm returning your call,' I reply.

Silence, and then 'It's Lesley, Adam's ex.' I feel angry but also nervous.

'Ah, okay, so why do you keep phoning?'

'I've, um, got some of Adam's things and I need to speak to him.' She's nervous. And bullshitting, I think. 'I'll ask him to call you,' I say, and put the phone down. I then feel bad for cutting her off. It's funny how our politeness even extends to people we don't like.

When Adam got home from work, I told him that Lesley had phoned. He looked surprised and nervous. Right, I think. She had him before, but I'm with him now. I convince him that he should remind her that it's over between them, as she clearly hasn't got the message.

Later that evening, I sit next to Adam as he dials Lesley's number.

'Lesley, it's me.' *Me*, I think. That's a bit familiar. They were supposed to have split up last year. How often do they speak?

'Don't phone here any more. No. Yes. No,' and he puts the phone down.

I can only imagine what she was saying on the other end of the phone. Her second question could have been, shall we meet up behind her back?

I am beginning to feel very territorial over Adam, and I don't like the feeling at all.

This morning, I have woken up to the sound of the phone ringing. It rings off before I reach it, but I feel sure it was Lesley calling. It rings again half an hour later and I scream down the phone 'Fuck off!' I only hope it wasn't someone else. I really do hope that she has got the message.

Later, I get back from work and Adam is not home yet. There is nothing to make a meal with in the fridge, so I decide to go shopping for a nice dinner for tonight. Cooking is completely new to me, so I need to make something simple but tasty. Later I am standing by the meat aisle in Waitrose, a shop I can't afford to buy very much in at all, but I'm drawn to it. I feel a tap on the shoulder. My heart leaps. I swing round quickly and see Luke, a friend from the past.

'Hello stranger,' he says, smiling. My God, his smile is gorgeous.

'Wow! Hello Luke!' We exchange a quick hug, and he smells gorgeous, musky and just, well, manly.

Luke is a classic bad boy, gorgeous looking, very funny and cheeky, but bad. We have never gone out with each other as boyfriend and girlfriend, but we have flirted with each other on and off for years. The type of girls that Luke goes for are different to me, certainly wilder. I remember him telling me, a few years ago, during a rare heart-to-heart, that he had always felt that he was inherently "bad". He admitted that he got so bored and frustrated doing normal 9-5 work, and that he liked to get money quickly and loved the excitement of crime.

I abandoned the steak that I had in my basket, feeling naughty, as I was new to this grocery shopping lark and felt like a fraud as it was, like a child doing adult things. We left the supermarket together and went to the nearest pub.

Although a local, I hadn't been in this particular pub before. He went to get our drinks at the bar, and I sat at a grubby little table in the corner. The décor was classic old man's pub, with a garish maroon patterned carpet and trinkets covering every available space. The juke box was playing 'Step On' by The Happy Mondays, which I guess that Luke had put on as it is his type of music. He came back to the table with a vodka and Coke for me and a cider for himself.

'So,' he says, smiling. 'What's going on in your life, then?'

I hesitate, as a part of me would like to pretend I don't have a boyfriend, but I say, 'I've actually moved in with Adam Johnson.' They knew each other from school.

'Really? Ah, he's a nice bloke. Where d'you meet him, then?' Luke had not gone to Anna's funeral, so I explained that I had met Adam at her funeral.

I had met Luke at a party a good few years ago, when I was around sixteen. He was popular with the girls, and a bit too dangerous for me. He was one of those boys that was everywhere you went, be it the local park or a nightclub. But I remember always having been excited to see him.

We catch up for over two hours, and although I'm having a really good time, I tell him I must go because Adam will be wondering where I am, and I don't want him calling my mum and worrying her.

As I put the key in the front door, Adam practically drags me in with the door which he is opening at the same time.

'Where the fuck have you been?'

I decide to be honest and explain that I had bumped into Luke.

He rubs his hand over his head.

'For fuck's sake, he's trouble! You know that!'

'Well,' I say, feeling childish, 'Tell your fucking ex to stop phoning *our* home!' I stomp off to bed. I wish I had stayed out with Luke. And, more than that, I wish that I had never moved in with Adam. He's not a nice person.

How did I not see that? You did. You just ignored it.

5

I am chopping carrots and onions to go in tonight's cottage pie, listening to Massive Attack's 'Unfinished Sympathy' on Radio One, feeling relaxed. The DJ refers to the group as "Massive", apparently because we are going to war in the Gulf and using the word "attack" seems inappropriate. This seems bizarre to me.

I think of Adam and our own little "love" war. One of our many incompatibilities are our nighttime habits, as I have always gone to bed early and Adam is a true night owl. We try to compromise by snuggling up together when I go to bed relatively early. Then Adam says goodnight, gets half-dressed and goes back to the front room to continue his evening.

However, often, when Adam eventually comes to bed, mayhem starts. As he walks into the bedroom, I instantly wake up and start to scream and panic, as if he is a masked murderer. After my screaming fit, I don't have any memory at all of what has disturbed me.

The underlying problem may well be my nighttime visitor, whom I haven't told Adam about. But I am always forewarned when my visitor comes, so how can I not distinguish between the visitor and my living breathing boyfriend? This is an ongoing issue and the only way to stop it is to go to bed at the same time, but Adam can't go to sleep early, and I can't stay up. When I think back to ex-boyfriends, we didn't live together so it was never an issue. Should he adapt for me, or I for him? I honestly don't have the answer.

Last night's dream wasn't too bad at all, as my dreams go. I remember looking in a huge mirror with Layla standing beside me and then we had some type of terrible argument in the street. Compared to the horrific dreams that I have recently been having, this feels very tame, so I didn't bother noting it down. If anyone ever get hold of my dream diary, I think I would be taken away and put in a padded cell.

The doorbell rings, breaking my thought pattern and I head to the door, excited to see Layla, and excited for her to see my little flat. It's always nice to see her and even more so right now as Adam is quite morose, so Layla's friendly face and demeanour is especially welcome. We sit together on the sofa, catching up, talking over each other in our excitement to fill each other in with everything that's gone on, then I show her round the tiny flat, which takes minutes. Adam and I don't have the spare money to spruce the place up so, apart from a coat of white paint, the furniture is all begged and borrowed.

Layla and I are wearing very similar outfits, jeans and black roll necks and our hairstyles, if you could call them that, are the same, long and natural. I desperately want the short pixie cut that Winona Ryder has, but I am not the pixie type. I think Layla could carry it off, though.

I hear a key in the front door. Adam is back from seeing a friend. He didn't tell me which friend he was seeing, and I didn't ask. He wanders into the front room and he looks seriously stoned, his face a green/yellow hue and his eyes completely bloodshot. I feel embarrassed, as this is the first time that Layla has met him. He knew she was coming; is that why he is playing up? Even through his stoned haze he can see that I'm not impressed, so he makes an effort to talk to Layla.

The evening is going okay, despite my initial worries, so, after eating, we decide to go the pub. We arrive at The King's Head, the popular pub for our age group now. The place is heaving with Friday night revellers and resembles a sea of denim and leather jackets. It takes forever to get a drink, so Adam orders double vodkas for us to save queuing again for a while. Both Layla and I have small bottles of Smirnoff vodka in our handbags, to allow for cheap top-ups. We have a good evening and a few of Adam's friends gather round Layla, who is flirting and enjoying herself. Blasting from the speakers dotted around the ceiling, Kenny Thomas' 'Thinking About Your Love', which gets everyone in the mood.

When Adam and his friends group together and seem to be otherwise distracted, I take the chance to pop to the ladies with Layla to find out what she makes of

Adam. We touch our lipstick up in the mirror, and I look at her reflection.

'So... what do you think?' I ask, smiling and thinking she will like him. She swings round to face me, and I think, Oh no. Layla has an almost pitiful look on her face.

'He's not for you.' '

'Huh?' I reply, dumbfounded.

'Look, he's too... I don't know, um... angry?' It comes out as a question, but we both know it is a fact.

'Ah well, it's only temporary,' I say, gathering myself together and trying to come across as relaxed about the whole situation. *She's probably jealous,* I think. *Of what, exactly?* My sensible inner voice always challenges my stupidity.

We go back into the pub, order another drink and, to the sounds of Adamski's 'Killer', we work our way through the crowds and eventually rejoin Adam and his friends. I can see that Adam is now flat out drunk, slurring his words, being downright rude, and I decide that it's time we headed home.

As we start to say our goodbyes, I spot Lesley walking her way through the crowd towards our group, like a cruise missile. She blanks me and hones in on Adam. I watch to see how he reacts. She whispers something to him, and he smiles and kisses her on the cheek. Layla is oblivious as she doesn't know Lesley.

Adam doesn't even glance at me, as if I am not there, or insignificant. I am so angry with both, Adam for being ignorant and Lesley for being sly. I have a strong feeling that their relationship is not finished, but I will bring it up with him when he is sober, whenever that may be.

On the walk home, I think back to how stoned Adam was earlier on. Layla and I are admittedly tipsy, but whenever Adam mixes cannabis with alcohol, he goes too far. As I walk along next to Layla, Adam starts to goad her and they squabble about who knows more about me, of all things. Adam's comments are getting increasingly barbed, and Layla is not holding back either. Then, suddenly, Adam grabs Layla in what is supposed to be a jokey headlock, but certainly doesn't feel that way. Even though tipsy, I push him away and I catch a look in his eyes that I don't like. He is jealous of Layla, not the other way round, I think. How can you be jealous of your partner's friends? He has enough friends of his own. I suppose, in his mind, she takes away my attention from him. I can't get my head around it.

Once Layla has headed home in a cab, I start clearing away the remains of the dinner in the kitchen. Adam walks in, attempting to walk steadily but failing miserably. As he pours himself a pint of water, I say 'Why don't you like Layla?'

He doesn't look at me, and as he walks off, he replies, 'I just don't,' sounding like a grumpy child.

I like most of Adam's friends and I honestly can't see anything not to like about Layla. But you would think that, she's your friend. Ah well, I think, I'll keep them separate. Yet another warning sign that our relationship is probably not going to work.

Despite my plan to wait until Adam is sober to confront him, I can't hold it in, so follow him into the front room and ask, 'So, what's going on with you and Lesley?' He reels round and walks towards me in his idiotic, drunk way.

'Nothing. She said hello, that's all.'

He looks furious, as if I have no right to ask him such an impertinent question. I look at him in disgust. I can't stand looking at him when he is drunk and pathetic. At this point, I don't care if something is going on between them. She can have him with my blessings.

It's as if the good times are already behind us and we have only been in a relationship for about six weeks. Why did I move in with him?

What was I thinking? *You weren't.*

6

It's early March, and our arguments continue. They say it takes two to argue and I realise that I am partly at fault. Everything that Adam does seems to irritate me. His flippant comments, his ignorance, his drinking. Where's the funny, cheeky guy that I fell for?

Every weekday, when he finishes work, he goes straight to the pub and, by the time he gets home, he has had a few too many drinks. He's not a mean drunk, but as I am sober, which is about 99% of the time, it is frustrating talking to someone whose speech slurs. We have an argument, we make up, we make the effort. Then, things fall apart. And so, the circle continues. It's crazy to think that we have only been together for two months.

I suppose in response to this, I seem to be comfort eating a bit too much. Stopping off at the baker's during my lunch hour is becoming way too commonplace. I feel tearful and over-dramatic and just not myself.

Yesterday evening, Adam had invited over his friend, Darren, whom I have known for a long time, way longer than I have known Adam. He's a nice enough guy, funny and with a kind nature. Because I wanted to make a real effort, I went to the shops earlier in the day and picked up every herb and spice I could find, along with some chicken fillets and rice, and I attempted to make a curry for the first time. I followed a recipe from a cookbook that my mum gave to me and tried not to get greasy fingerprints on the huge weighty tome. I'm not finding this cooking lark particularly easy, or enjoyable for that matter, and I really don't think I'm a natural cook. But I persevere, as it seems to be the thing to do.

Adam and Darren strolled in at around eight p.m., by which time I was hungry and a bit annoyed that they had stayed in the pub so long. But then we sat down to eat and chat and laugh. The food seemed to go down well, but I find it difficult to critique my own food. And then, as soon as Adam had finished eating and had put his cutlery down, he pushed his chair back and announced, almost proudly, 'We're off to the pub again.'

I was aghast.

'Are you joking?' I asked, thinking, *please be joking*. I looked to Darren, who looked embarrassed, and back at Adam, who just stood there looking cocky, with a mean look on his face. Something in me snapped and I just completely lost my head. I started to launch glass bowls, plates, cups, cutlery and everything I could lay my hands on at the walls of the kitchen, leaving no white space untouched. Adam and Darren didn't say a word, they just got out of the kitchen quickly and then I heard the front door slam. I sat down on a kitchen chair and started to cry my heart out. There was curry and broken glass over every surface, just a complete mess. I thought *What is wrong with me. Is that a normal reaction?*

After about half an hour of crying, I still couldn't believe their behaviour. They ate the meal that I slaved over for hours and swiftly left. But I *did* overreact. And sadly, I then had a load of mess to clear up because there was no way on earth that Adam would have helped. As I started the horrible job of clearing up the mess from my extreme temper tantrum, Elton John and George Michael belted out 'Don't Let the Sun Go Down on Me' on the little stereo player in the kitchen, which certainly didn't help my tears to stop flowing. I felt very sorry for myself.

When Adam came back from the pub, he kept away from me and I steered clear of him. He slept on the sofa and, predictably, that night the nightmares came. I had one of what I call my "epic" dreams, very long and involved, playing out like a blockbuster film with a huge cast of people and many adventures.

I remember being in my old home and spotting horrendous looking spiders all over the house. Some childhood friends were in the "epic" and we were all travelling in a huge bus which was being followed by the police, as somehow there had been a murder and we were under suspicion. I remember being sick, but as is often the case lately, I am too tired in the morning to bother writing anything down, so I only remember parts of the dream.

Following my plate-smashing meltdown, we don't speak to each other for a couple of days. And I thaw first. *I will not give in. I will not give in.* I give in. I apologise for overreacting, and ask Adam to apologise for being ignorant, which he does, reluctantly. I suggest that we make a nice night of it and watch a good film on video together.

Adam goes over to Blockbusters and brings back a couple of films, *Arachnophobia* and *The Abyss*, a sci-fi horror. Adam knows that I like scary films, but *Arachnophobia* is a step too far as I am terrified of spiders. So that is the film we started with, as he said he thought I should confront my fear and it could cure me. It didn't. But we enjoyed it, Adam laughing at my screams and laughter.

We ate taramasalata and pita bread, perhaps my effort to recreate our little indoor picnic from when we first met. We enjoy the second film, whilst sipping Malibu with pineapple juice and have a nice evening, back to being friends again.

When the films have finished, I think back to when Adam bought me the video player and I feel warmth towards him. He comes to bed with me, and we start to cuddle. I'm so pleased that we are getting on again; it can be so lonely when you live with someone but are both doing the silent treatment.

Then, suddenly, I feel nauseous.

'Oh no…' I run to the bathroom and just make it in time, vomiting down the toilet time and again. Adam comes in and lightly pats my back a bit pathetically. When there is nothing left in me, I have a bath and get into bed. It must have been the taramasalata, maybe it was off. But Adam seems fine.

What is up with me?

It is Tuesday in the early evening, and I am lying on my bed following an after-work nap. When we moved in together, I told Adam about *Twin Peaks*, a spooky American TV series. The show is about a missing girl, Laura Palmer. It is twisted, dark and very strange, quite like my dreams, so it fascinates me. But there's a character in it called Bob who scares the life out of me. As soon as there's any indication that Bob is about to show up in the programme, I avert my eyes. This evening we are planning to continue watching the second season together. It's on BBC2 at nine p.m. every Tuesday, so straight after work I have a nap on a Tuesday, to allow me to stay up later.

I have been going to bed earlier and earlier. I wonder if I might be depressed. I think back to my dream of Bob last week. I dreamt of him because I have been watching *Twin Peaks*, as simple as that. Why do I watch scary stuff? It's not helpful, or is it? I had read somewhere that the type of film that you watch is replacing something that is missing in your life. That is certainly not the case with me. I can't work it out myself, but the closest way that I can explain it to Layla is that I am trying to scare myself so much and experience every horror so that nothing can then scare me in my dreams. And I seem to be constantly looking for answers.

Bob seems to be in this series a lot more than the last. When the programme has finished, I ask Adam to stay with me until I'm asleep. We are getting on fine now, and that old spark is back.

Also, on the plus side, Lesley hasn't called for a while. Maybe she has given up on Adam now. I hope so. Luke called the other evening and Adam came in the front room as I spoke to him. Luke asked if we could meet up in Camden the following weekend and have a day out together, but although it pained me, I turned him down gently, saying that I want to make a go of it with Adam. Maybe we can make a go of this.

In the morning, I am over the moon that Bob didn't enter my dreams, and for a nice change, I seemed to sleep well, with no nightmares, no unwanted visitors and no memories of anything scary. I can't think why I had a restful night, but I hope this continues, and I hope that the visitor has disappeared, as he did last time. I am wide awake and feeling refreshed at six a.m.

7

I have decided that I need a girls' night away from Adam.

It's Saturday, late afternoon, and as I get ready for this evening, I feel uncomfortable in my jeans. All this comfort eating is starting to show. My jeans feel tight around my thighs and stomach which irritates me so much. I tie a jumper round my waist to hide the area, but I'm still irritated. When's the last time I had a period? It hasn't been recently. In fact, I don't think it's been since I moved in with Adam a couple of months ago. But I'm on the pill, so I can't be pregnant.

I then think of the little girl and boy in my dream recently. I probably dreamt of having children because I have moved out, so I suppose it's a natural progression to consider. But not in a relationship like ours. In fact, thinking about it, I don't ever remember dreaming of Adam. Maybe he is insignificant, I think. I hope so. I know we have sexual chemistry, and he makes me laugh. But I don't like him very much at all.

I arrive at the pub in a cab. It's the first time I've been here, and it is a nice surprise, both the décor and the feel of the place. It seems a bit posher than our usual pub, but not stuffy. It's now nine p.m. and the pub is busy, although not as jam-packed as our locals would be. I spot Layla with her mum and another lady sitting on a raised seating area and go over to join them.

Layla's mum, Deana, introduces me to her friend, Kath, who seems nice, if a bit girly and giggly. I have always been a bit wary of Deana, and I can't quite put my finger on it. She's into tarot cards and all sorts of hippy type things and is supposed to be spiritual. I don't even know what that means. Tonight, she has pink and purple streaks in her hair, but mixed with the grey hairs. I don't like the look as I think she looks too old for punky hair. It's like she is trying to be as young as Layla, and I find it irritating and a bit desperate. I feel mean thinking this. But she rubs me up the wrong way.

We all dip our straws in to a huge goblet filled with some type of sickly-sweet cocktail. Deana paid, so even though it tastes over sweet and pretty rank, Layla and I go for it, as it will save us some money. Deana and Kath, despite being twice our age, start to get embarrassingly loud and drunk, so Layla and I sneak off without being noticed. I order us a couple of white wines, if only to get rid of the sweet cocktail which is literally coating my teeth. We find somewhere else to sit and watch the funny antics going on. A group of men are desperately trying to flirt with some uninterested females, and we watch and laugh at their failed attempts.

'Does this wine taste horrible to you?' I ask Layla, already knowing she will say no, as she is knocking it back happily.

'No, it tastes fine to me.' Maybe it's the cocktail from earlier that has made this taste bitter in comparison. I can't finish it, so give the rest to Layla.

As the night nears its end, Layla says 'Let's head back to find Mum and Kath.' I really don't want to be in Deana's company. Usually, I can tolerate her, but something is telling me to stay away from her. It is an instinctual feeling. Get away! But how do I explain this to Layla? I can't. That's her mum.

When we find them, they are deep in drunken conversation with a couple of old-looking men squashed into the seats with them. *Come on Layla, let's leave them to it,* I think. Layla just rolls her eyes, and we climb into the leather sofa seats directly next to them. I try to drown them out as the loud, drunken flirting goes on and concentrate on enjoying my time with Layla.

Then, suddenly, above the noise of the music, I can hear some sort of commotion coming from Deana. I look over to her and she's pointing directly at me and the man next to her is trying to pull her arm back and trying to shush her.

'Huh?' I say, not hearing clearly or understanding what she is trying to get at. '

'You've got a black shadow hanging over you,' she slurs. My heart rate rises, and I feel angry. Stupid drunk woman.

Layla says, 'Shut up, Mum, you're drunk!'

'What is she on about?'

I turn to Layla, and she says, 'Come on, ignore her, she's totally pissed.'

But what frightens me is that I catch the frightened look in Deana's eyes. Layla leads me away by the arm as we walk away towards the entrance. As I turn back to look at Deana again, she is arguing with the man and trying to point at me again, the man having none of it, pulling her arm back, trying to calm her down.

Outside in the freezing air, we are dressed for the warmer weather, no coats, just thin roll-neck tops and jeans. We huddle together and talk about anything apart from her mum. But it bugs me.

Have I got a black cloud over me?

1990

1989

1988

1987

1986

1985

PART SIX
14 YEARS OLD

1984 – 35 years ago
1

A group of us are milling about in the street at nighttime. The road we are in is not familiar and is very posh-looking. The houses are very tall and there are no lights on inside, the only source of light is an old-fashioned looking streetlamp. Lit up by the glow of the lamp, we see a group of people in dark uniforms ahead, outside one of the houses. We know something is happening, so we hold back to see what is going on.

Suddenly, there is a flurry of activity. Anna grabs hold of my arm and points towards an upper window of the house, and I see a foreign man pointing a gun out of the window at what we now realise are policemen. The gunman shoots and a policeman falls on the floor. Anna and I are scared to move closer, but Si moves nearer to the group who are crouching over the injured man. Si calls back, 'It's a policewoman!' We are frightened and start to run, as a group, back the way we came from.

We find ourselves in a park. It looks like our normal park but is a nicer version. It is so posh, like a royal park, with a large green space and carefully tended shrubs. Anna is with us, along with Helena and Si.

Si starts to run over to an abandoned children's train which is oddly placed in the middle of the park. It snakes round in an S shape. It doesn't give me a good feeling; it feels spooky but childish somehow, with carriages the shape of fairground Waltzers.

We all catch up with Si and start to assemble by the carriages. A man appears from nowhere and I realise that he oversees the train and has come to collect money from us. He is the actor from *Blackadder* who plays Baldrick and I wonder why he's charging us as he must be rich, as he's famous. I don't have any cash on me, so I hand him some Monopoly money and he doesn't seem to realise it is fake.

I climb in to the second carriage, as I somehow know to keep the front carriage free for someone, but I don't know who. I sit next to Anna, but she is not her normal happy self; she seems sad about something, but she won't talk so I don't know what is making her unhappy.

The train jolts and then starts to chug along very slowly, but not on any rails, just directly on the grass. I wonder what is powering the train but I kind of know that this is a dream. I hope the chairs don't spin. I look behind at the others and feel a jolt of fright as I see that John the twin is covered in blood, all over the front of his white T-shirt. But he smiles and raises his cup and I realise with relief that he has dropped his Slush Puppie all over himself.

In the carriage behind John there's a dark-haired girl sitting on her own. I haven't seen her before, but I don't ask the others who she is. I realise that they can't see her, only I can. The train starts to slow down, and I feel a jolt of fright as I realise we are now entering the scary bridge in Dane Road. The grimy grey brick walls are lined with tall, slim mirrors. I can't bear to look, but I don't want to act scared in front of the others because they are oblivious to the danger and all laughing and enjoying themselves, so I look downwards into my lap.

Something catches my eye, and I look up to see Matt sitting in the carriage in front of us and he starts to look round at me slowly, too slowly. I know what I will see before I see it, so I look away, but as I turn my head to the side, I catch a glimpse of his evil smiling face. Don't look! I shut my eyes and when I open them, I'm relieved to see that both Matt and the mirrors have gone but there is someone hidden behind the brick wall, throwing huge amounts of water over us. Is this part of the ride? Everyone else seems to be having fun, so it must be. We are all getting drenched, and I look down and see that my canvas boots are soaked through. The water keeps on coming and is drenching us all. I see that, in amongst the water, a bunch of red roses has landed on my lap. I throw them off on to the floor of the carriage, as they don't feel nice; they have the unpleasant feel of something that is dirty, almost like someone is mocking me.

The train rolls to a stop, still under the dream bridge which I notice is much wider than the real bridge, and we all climb out of the carriages to get ourselves dry. We then sit under huge individual hairdryers that are lined up in a row.

I now find myself outside a house that I haven't seen before. It is tall and old-fashioned looking, and kind of squished. Although I don't know the house, it feels like a haven.

I wake up from my eerie dream and almost instantly feel a sense of pure dread. This feeling is way worse than watching any horror film. Worse than *The Exorcist*? Don't think about that! Something bad is in my bedroom with me. I can't see anything, but I know it's here. *Mum! Dad!* I try to scream out, but I can't talk. It's like I've been drugged. My whole body is frozen, apart from my eyes, and there's a loud buzzing in my ears. I'm awake because I can see my Michael Jackson posters and I can also see my alarm clock clearly. It's 1.06 a.m. I squeeze my eyes shut tight, in fear. *Wake up, wake up, wake up.*

Now, I feel the cover pulled off my feet. From the end of the bed, someone or something crawls up under the covers. Who or what? I feel a heavy weight on my body, and I can't fight it off. The weight is on my arms, legs and chest, and then, I can feel it inside me, oh God. I can feel hot breath on my face and down below it feels … Not pain, more like pressure. Breathe. It's not real. I remember this feeling. But from when? I try to open my eyes a tiny bit, even though I am frightened to see what is on me.

What I see makes my heart hammer like it's going to jump right out of my chest. It looks like Matt, lying on top of me, staring right at me. But it's not. The thing's face is like Matt's but morphed into an evil version. I shut my eyes again and keep them tightly shut. I know it's not Matt. It's something pretending to be him.

Please leave me alone…

2

I woke up this morning in a foul mood. My dreams last night have upset me and there is no way I am going to school. But I must admit, it doesn't take very much at all for me to bunk school. It really does make the week go faster.

Mum comes in to wake me up for the third time and I try to make my voice sound as croaky as possible, as I peep my head out of the covers. Also, I keep my eyes closed from the moment I wake up which somehow makes me sound more tired.

'I've got a sore throat.' I'm nicely surprised at how croaky my voice does sound, probably helped by the fact that I haven't been awake for long.

'Okay.' Mum sighs. 'Just try to drink lots of water today and I'll see you later.'

Mum's answer to everything is water but I find it completely tasteless. I have always found it weird that we drink something that is used to bathe in.

I can never tell if Mum knows that I am having her on, but she is distracted today as she is running late for work, so she just closes my bedroom door. Listening carefully to hear what's going on in the rest of the house,

I hear my sister's muffled voice asking Mum questions and Mum being a bit snappy with her.

I soon hear the front door close as Mum heads off to drop Alice to school on her way to work. Mum's work is half an hour's drive away, so she rarely comes home during school hours. I now have the entire house to myself, as Dad leaves super early to get the train to work. I don't know how he does it.

I give it about two minutes, which seems like ages, and then leap out of bed. I grab a pencil and a pad and start to write down everything I can remember from my dream, and as I do, I start to remember more about the waking dream of the demonic presence pretending to be Matt.

What does it all mean? Is there an actual ghost who is tormenting me? Or am I going a bit mad? Dad has moaned about mine and Mum's "bloody hormones". Could it be that mine are wrong somehow and are making me ill in the head? Dad even recently bought a huge box full of Evening Primrose Oil to calm our monthly moods that come with our periods.

I must cut my dream notes short as Anna is due round soon. Our plan, which has worked for us every time so far, is for Anna to wait at the station bridge at the top of the road for me, and when I join her and we see my mum's car drive past, then we know that we are in the clear, and head to mine. If, like today, I don't turn up, she knows I am pretending to be unwell, and she still heads to mine on her own. She will have gone into the little sweet shop alone and bought four cigarettes, for 40p, which we call "singles", from the old man who works there. Four is just enough for us as we don't have much money and we don't want to smell of smoke. We smoke Consulate, as they are mint flavour so not as potent smelling as some cigarettes.

When we get to mine, we never waste any time, and we start our day of bunking off by exploring the fridge and cupboards to see what we can eat without Mum and Dad knowing we were here in the day.

Recently, I tried mixing dry Paxo stuffing mix with boiling water and it was disgusting. Angel's Delight is always a good choice as Mum never seems to notice when that goes missing, and butterscotch flavour is the ultimate treat. Our second favourite food to take is eggs if there are a load of them. We gather a few each and go up to the train station, stand on the bridge, and throw eggs at passing trains. Although we haven't done that recently, as my mum keeps noticing that the eggs are disappearing quickly, so we have had to lay off that for a while.

We go in the back garden when we smoke our cigarettes and hide down by the cellar door, which isn't overlooked by any nosey neighbours. When we have finished, we place the disgusting smelly cigarette butts through a hole in the fence. The incredibly old lady next door has a very overgrown garden so she will never notice them. In fact, they probably won't get discovered until the lady dies and new people move in and clear the jungle-like garden. I hope she lives a very long life.

At about two thirty, we leave the house and go to the park which is about five minutes' walk away. This is great in the summer, but not so much fun in the winter. Then, at around three thirty, we slowly head home. It is always easy to trick Mum when she gets home from picking up Alice from primary school.

'How was school?' Mum always asks.

I always relate a story to her about something that did, in fact, happen at school on a day that I was there, so I'm not actually lying, as such.

The only annoying thing about our bunking off school is that we must still wear our stupid school uniform. The uniform is maroon, which is the worst colour that I can ever imagine. Why? Just why? Green would be worse.

After 'school', I start to get ready for my night out. I need to dress casually tonight as we will be in a muddy field, so I wear my Benneton off-the-shoulder top and baggy turned-up jeans.

Later, in the evening, we walk across the dark field towards the fair. The atmosphere is exciting with the combination of the bright lights flashing and the music blaring. I can begin to smell the burgers and then the candy floss as we get closer, and we hear the screams of the kids on the Meteoroid. I won't be going on that, as I am a chicken when it comes to fairground rides. I am only brave enough to go on the Waltzers, and even they make me feel sick.

'Whoa, ghost train!' says Si, speeding up ahead in his excitement. The ghost train has a huge frontage painted with some scary and some not so scary, monsters, but it's the actual train carriages that stir something within me and I think back to my dream. There's no way I can dodge going on the ghost train, I would get teased too much. The lights on the frontage are mostly green and red, and the huge iron gates on the outside of the carriages are shaped like cobwebs. On closer inspection, the main zombie-looking monster painted in the centre of the frontage is quite nasty and will probably crop up tonight in my dreams.

Some of the boys, along with Helena and Alex, head to the bumper cars, which I don't have much interest in. The rest of us gather near the Waltzers, and all pile into carriages as soon as the last passengers have got off. In some cases, while they are still getting off. I share a carriage with Anna and notice that the man running the Waltzer has his eye on us. *Oh no,* I think. *He's going to really spin us round a lot.* And he does.

When we stagger off, I struggle to stop myself from being sick and I feel the need for something sweet, so I buy a huge candy floss. The other's buy burgers and hot dogs and we sit on a patch of grass and watch the goings-on. Helena has her Kodak disposable camera at the ready, and we all pose for the photo, pulling silly faces. I notice that the outfit I am wearing almost matches with Helena's, but she is tiny, whereas I am tall, so luckily, we don't look like identikits of each other.

We walk around the fair, stopping and talking to other friends we come across. Then we find ourselves back at the ghost train. I feel nervous to go on it, but I must join in as all the others are so keen. My dream comes back to me, with an image of Matt sitting in the front carriage, so I am relieved to see Si climb into the front carriage with Helena. I'm pleased that the reality is at least different in this way. Matt is not even at the fair, as he has football training tonight. I hold back to let others climb in, and I get into the fourth carriage with John the twin, the carriage where the dark-haired girl was sitting in my dream.

The train starts to move slowly towards the entrance to the ride, and my stomach starts to clench up, making me feel queasy. But within moments of entering the gaping clown's mouth serving as the entrance, as it turns out, the ride is not scary at all. The others are having so much fun, screaming and laughing at the 'monsters' popping out, they don't notice that I am sitting quietly.

It's getting late and we have run out of money, so we all head home. I decide to bite the bullet and go the normal way home, rather than go miles out of my way. As I approach the scary bridge, I resign myself to whatever is waiting for me. I trudge through, feeling tired and fed up. I have no fear at all walking through the bridge, for the first time ever. Because this is just a bridge. And I am so tired.

It's tiring being afraid all the time.

3

Saturday morning, my hair scrunched up with nearly half a tube of Studio Line gel, I meet up with friends, all girls, and we walk along together on our way to the train station. Mum had remarked, sarcastically that it was a miracle how my sore throat had cleared up so quickly. I think, but don't dare say, that sarcasm is the lowest form of wit.

The weather has started to warm up and the sun is shining for what feels like the first time this year. The houses in this road are huge posh houses with super neat gardens and, mostly, more than one car in their drives. I love walking up this road and imagining that I can pick any house I want to live in.

My favourite house is halfway up and, on the left, set quite far back from the road and down a huge sloping drive. The shrubs in huge terracotta pots outside the front door are so perfect that they look fake. But they must be real because there are petals scattered around the base of the pots. The thing that fascinates me the most are the huge windows that go from the upstairs to the downstairs, and you can see right in, no net curtains even. I've never seen anyone on the staircase. In fact, I don't think I've ever seen anyone outside their house in this road. It seems like rich people are never home. Maybe they are too busy earning money.

We walk along in a group, all but one of us, Anna, wearing our *Frankie Says Relax* T-shirts. I don't like wearing T-shirts as they are not clingy enough, but I will wear this one. Anna has on a plain purple top. She usually does her own thing when it comes to clothes and I kind of like her more because of that. I tell my friends about my house-choosing game and they all join in. Alex picks out my favourite house, so we agree that we will live in it together. We joke about walking down the stairs with no clothes on to shock people walking past.

We arrive at the train station and buy some sweets and Slush Puppies from the little kiosk just inside the front entrance. We are mucking around, and Jane manages to drop her whole drink down her Frankie top. We are all crying with laughter. Even Jane, but not as much as the rest of us.

We get on the Northern Line train, headed for Tottenham Court Road, our new favourite destination. There is an amusement arcade that we like going to, to play the games and to meet new boys. But today there's not much going on there, so we decide to leave the arcade and jump on the bus to Covent Garden. As we are about to leave, a couple of grown men start trying to chat us up and Anna gets offered a lift in one of their cars, but we drag her off with us and head to the bus stop.

As soon as we get off the bus, we come across a small crowd. We squeeze our way to the front, and in the centre, there are a group of guys taking it in turns to body pop and break dance. It's such fun to watch all their moves and we love the music they are dancing to. Our group of boys that we hang around with do try to dance like that, but seeing these guys in action, I think our boys need some practice to be able to impress us girls.

Alex is really into her dancing, so we go to look for Pineapple Dance Studios. However, when we find it, we are all too embarrassed to go inside, mainly because of Jane's bright-blue-stained top, so we just hang about outside waiting to see any dancers come out. When we tire of this, we get some hot dogs from a stand and get on a bus to who knows where, jumping off at St. James' Square.

We end up in a beautiful posh park, or gardens, remind me of the flowers scene in *Oliver*, with the grand white buildings surrounding the green. The song 'Who Will Buy' jumps into my mind. The square also reminds me of my dream the other night, with the huge white buildings all joined together. There are very few people about, which is a sweet relief after the hustle and bustle of Covent Garden, so we sit on a bench and eat our hot dogs. We devour our lunch, barely talking.

When we have eaten, we attempt to climb on a huge horse statue and as none of us are athletic, we end up on the grass, laughing until we cry. The occasional posh person walking past with a dog gives us disapproving looks, which makes us laugh more. This was probably the ghastliest thing that ever happened to their super posh neighbourhood. I sincerely doubt that there is ever any crime or drama around here.

We have a big night ahead of us, so we get on the tube and head home early in the afternoon. When we reach our stop, we go our separate ways to head home, so that we can get ready for tonight. We are all excited as there is a house party at Mark's, as his mum and dad have gone away for Easter, luckily for us. Mark is quite a new friend as he only joined our school about six months ago. He came from a school in Southgate, about fifteen minutes away, and was instantly popular with our group. This seems to be the case with new boys in general. His old school is supposedly our rival, but I have never seen any fights or trouble between the two, so I think that it is just talk.

I start getting ready as soon as I get home at dinner time. Well, dinner time for people that are not on a diet. I like to take hours to put my make-up on and try out different colours. My hair takes ages too. Shampoo makes my hair too smooth, and I want it all big and messy, so I sneak into Mum's room and use loads of her Elnett hairspray and then back-comb my hair like crazy. It is a bit frightening because it will be so knotty tomorrow, but it's worth it for tonight.

I turn around in the full-length mirror on the front of my wardrobe, checking that my outfit looks perfect.

I have a fear of mirrors in the dark, but it is still light outside. I briefly think of my worst recurring dream, my evil reflection in the back room patio doors. But looking in the mirror in the daytime is safe, so far.

I'm wearing my black mini skirt with a huge chunky belt diagonally over my hips, and a long white vest with a bright pink string vest over the top. I have styled myself to look like Madonna. If only I had a huge cross necklace to finish the look.

Finally, I am ready, so I call the others and we arrange to meet at the park bandstand. Walking to meet them, my feet start to hurt and, by the time I get to the park, my white canvas boots are hurting my feet so much and my heels are bleeding. This is the first time I have worn them, and I regret not wearing them in, but I never remember to. I take them off, with difficulty, as they are probably a size too small, and Helena tries to stretch them for me. We all join in at one point, pulling and twisting them, but they end up getting dirty, as Helena's hands are covered in foundation, so I decide to go barefoot.

We head off in our group of seven towards Mark's house and, as we pass the brook, I throw my boots in. Mum will be very cross as she only bought them for me in the week, and I had begged for them incessantly for about two weeks prior to that, but I will just say that someone stole them.

Our group this evening consists of three girls: me, Helena and Anna, and four boys: John the twin, Roly,

Gary and Si. I don't fancy any of the boys, but Anna likes Si, and he likes her too. Helena likes John the twin and he doesn't realise, even though I think she's made it obvious. He doesn't really get involved with any girls, so maybe he's just nervous. Tonight, she is going to tell him outright that she fancies him, so we are all waiting to see what happens.

I like Matt, and all my thoughts are taken up with thinking of him. I so hope he is at Mark's party tonight, as Matt goes to Mark's old school, but I have a feeling he won't be. He is a good-looking boy, with a dark brown wedge and he is a casual, so he always looks smart, not to mention grown-up. He's not quite as tall as me, but hardly any boys are. And men scare me a bit, so I stick to boys of my own age.

We arrive at Mark's house, excited and ready to party, armed with Woodpecker cider, beers and as many cigarettes as we could buy. In my handbag, I have a Soda Stream bottle filled with my favourite Martini Rosso, from Dad's drinks cabinet. I really don't know why he keeps a drinks cabinet, as I seem to be the only one that drinks from it. Although he doesn't know that.

There are a few people dotted around that I don't know, friends of Mark's from his old school. We dance around to 'Dr Beat' by Miami Sound Machine and muck around. Then some of the others decide to play spin the bottle, but I steer well clear because I don't fancy any of the boys in the house. Helena surprises me and doesn't play, and she quietly tells me, away from the others, that she doesn't want to be paired with anyone but John the twin. She also reveals that she has chickened out of telling him she wants to go out with him. I'm secretly relieved, as I think he would turn her down and I don't want her feelings to get hurt.

We kneel together on the floor near to the group playing spin the bottle and look through Mark's record collection. His records are clearly mixed up with his parents' collection and I spot a few albums that I secretly like but can never admit to, especially The Carpenters and The Bee Gees.

When the group are finished playing, Anna and I go into the garden to share a cigarette, as Mark has banned us from smoking inside. Even though everyone is loud, the music is louder, and whilst outside, we hear the familiar sound of Colonel Abrams' 'Trapped' come on the stereo. Our favourite song, we race into the front room and start dancing in a silly way, like we are robots.

When we get tired of dancing, we sit on the floor and chat to Si and Gary. Si is pouring Southern Comfort and Coke in to four mugs and passing them round. It doesn't taste so nice from a mug, somehow, but Mark has told us that his parents have no drinking glasses. I think he is lying, to save his parents' glasses, as he knows for sure that there will be some breakages.

Then Gary suggests getting the Ouija board out. *Oh no,* I think. Everyone else seems up for it, so I don't say much and pretend to go along with it initially, but when the board has been set up on the dining table and everyone has started to quieten down, I feel myself sober up somewhat and decide I don't want anything to do with it. I don't let on to my friends that I am afraid, so I make the excuse of feeling a bit queasy and drift off into the kitchen.

There is a girl sitting on a tall bar stool at the kitchen counter, with Hula Hoops on all her fingers. She is one of Mark's friends that I haven't met before, a short girl with shiny long black hair. I ask her if she is foreign. She tells me that her dad is from Egypt and her mum is English. We start to chat, and I learn that her name is Layla. She says she was named after some old group's song, and she hates her name. I think it's a lovely name, exotic sounding.

'I don't want to be involved in that,' Layla said, pointing towards where the group are sitting in the dining room, and she looked a bit sheepish.

'Me neither, I reply, relieved.

A moment's silence, and then, 'I believe in all that,' I said, nervously.

'Me too' Layla grinned, kind of sadly, and we locked eyes momentarily, an understanding passing between us. And so, just like that, our friendship was cemented.

Arriving home later, feeling quite drunk, I turn on every light switch that I pass, as Mum, Dad and Alice are at a party themselves, so I am home alone. I go upstairs to my bedroom and close my door. I lie on my bed, fully clothed; I'm tired, but my bedroom feels wrong somehow. Almost like it is buzzing with electricity. The alarm clock display is flickering, and I see it is 01.06 a.m. I pull the plug out of the wall.

Leave me alone, I think. I turn on the TV, the main ceiling light and my bedside lamp, flooding the room with light and sound and I fall asleep quickly.

4

We only have two days left at school before we break up for Easter. I love Easter but then I love every school holiday. I don't hate school, I just don't like getting up early. Especially recently, as my dreams have been real nightmares and I have started to sleepwalk again. My mum told me that I was a sleepwalker when I was young, which I don't have any memory of. I do remember my dreams though, unfortunately. The recurring dreams are the worst. I try not to dwell on them, and I try to push them to the back of my mind, concentrating on my friends and any boys that I like.

Even though I am only fourteen years old, I behave like I am much older, I think. I hate it when Mum and Dad say I am just a child. No, I'm not. They are so old now that they have forgotten how to have fun. But sometimes I do feel sad about getting older.

Dad recently got up in the loft and brought down loads of boxes filled with our old toys. As I sorted through my boxes, I felt a wave of sadness that I was having to grow up. I looked through my old Carrie dolls, Hobbie Hollie rag dolls and felt emotional when I saw my play treehouse. I loved this toy more than any other, the neat house with the little plastic people inside. I loved that you could close the house at night by pressing down the bright green plastic lid shaped as a tree, and I loved the feeling of protection and security it gave to my little people.

I don't know where it came from, but looking at my old toys, I got really upset and said to Mum, 'I get grown up stuff for Christmas and birthdays now, and I miss all this kind of stuff.' Mum comforted me and as she boxed everything back up, she agreed that nothing would be thrown away.

Part of me is still a little girl but part of me wants to grow up fast. All my group are desperate to leave school and go out to work as soon as possible, as we all want more money.

School days are spent sitting in each lesson and having one long endless discussion about boys, quietly, so the teachers don't hear. We also pass notes where possible, but Mr Kent, our English teacher, is incredibly strict so we don't dare do it in his class. We have our own system, whereby we write someone's name on a piece of paper, and the codes are a tick which means we fancy someone, a cross meaning we don't, a question mark if we are not sure, and an exclamation mark if someone is being embarrassing or stupid. The only important consideration during our average school day is who is going out with whom, why, how and when. I don't believe any of us concentrate in any of our lessons, apart from art class. I most certainly don't. Our hobbies are mostly buying make-up, drinking cider, or any alcohol we can lay our hands on, boyfriends and, our favourite pastime of all, house parties.

Straight after school, Alex and I get the bus to the town centre to look through the new albums at Our Price and then we head to Alex's, just four doors away from mine, for tea.

It's the first time I've been to Alex's house as she's a new friend and closer to Helena, whereas I'm closer to Anna. Alex's mum seems to like Spain as there are ornaments of donkeys wearing sombreros and little china Spanish dancers in gorgeous frilly dresses dotted all around the living room. I think Mum would hate this house. I will tell her all about it later.

When tea is served, I'm surprised to see that the food is so different to what I'm used to, but I love it. Findus Crispy pancakes with oven chips and for dessert a Hippo Pota Mousse. Mum makes old-fashioned food like roast dinners and chilli con carne, so I'm going to ask her to get some of the food that Alex's mum buys, as it is so tasty.

After tea, we get ready and, finally, it's time for us to head to the social club. Before we leave Alex's house, we creep into her mum's bedroom and spray lots of Lou Lou perfume all over us.

We meet Anna and Helena at the corner of the road, and we head off to the club together. As we walk down Dane Road, we come to the dreaded bridge. Whenever we walk under the bridge together, we always make a lot of noise to act like we are brave, but we then end up running the last little bit until we are back out in the open.

This evening, Anna dares us to walk silently all the way through. We are all giggling and grabbing each other's arms before we go in and, when we finally enter, all together, any thoughts of laughter disappear. My heart is hammering. We have made this more frightening, I think, realising I will have to walk through here alone later tonight. It's the huge brick wall to the side that frightens us the most, as we can't see what is on the other side, we can only imagine.

I picture every horror film monster standing the other side of the wall, waiting to catch us alone and drag us over the side like rag dolls, our faces frozen in silent screams. I imagine a whole host of monsters waiting to get me, depending on the evening I walk through. The werewolf from *American Werewolf in London*, Michael Myers from *Halloween*, Jason from *Friday the 13th* and Reagan from *The Exorcist*, to name a few. Time seems to slow down as we walk silently, but we reach the other side unscathed and successfully complete the dare.

I'm thinking I will probably go the long way home later, even though it takes me half an hour more. That, or I will just have to run through as fast as I can.

We arrive at the club and gather with our group. Every Wednesday, we meet at the 13-18's social club and the actual club is quite boring, but the boys like to play pool there. John the twin is showing off his amazing Rubik's Cube time, as he can match all the sides in one minute and fifty seconds, which is so impressive. But other than that, not much else is going on. The music is not great, and the hall is large and cold.

Every week, after the club, we all gather in the graveyard nearby and that is way more fun. We muck around and try to scare each other, and someone always seems to have something interesting with them. Tonight, one of the boys has brought a gas canister with him and is trying to get high on it. The boys all smoke JPS cigarettes which make me cough, so we try to make sure we have some Consulate or Silk Cut with us.

Helena tells us about a big news story that she watched on TV earlier on. Apparently, there was a siege carried out by Libyan men today, and a policewoman was shot and killed. This happened in St. James' Square, where we ate our lunch on Saturday. The place had looked so serene and posh. And then it comes back to me, my dream of a beautiful royal-looking park. And dreaming of a policewoman getting shot. But I can't think of it now because I'm enjoying myself too much.

When it gets late, we all head through the park and then go our separate ways. I decide to brave it and walk under the bridge rather than go the long way, but it is so dark. As I approach the bridge, nearly at the dreaded entrance, a man who has pulled out of the petrol station pulls up his car beside me. He winds down his window and I recognise him. He is a local man who hangs around in the village.

'Hello, gorgeous. Do you need a lift home?'

I am just about to decline and then I look ahead at the bridge and say, 'Yes.'

'Hop in, then,' he says, and I open the door and get into the passenger seat.

'You're Zoe, aren't you?' he asks.

'No. I'm Lisa.' I don't know why I lie to him.

He pulls away from the kerb and drive sunder the bridge. When he is nearly at my road, he points to it, then passes it, and says, 'So, if you're not Zoe, you don't live there then, do you?'

His smile is not nice, and I start to regret getting in his car.

'Can you just let me out?' I ask. 'I'll walk from here.' My panic is rising.

'Don't you want to go for a ride, get to know me?' he says, putting his hand on my knee. Not just rested there, gripping it.

'I've got to get home. My dad's a policeman and he's strict,' I lie.

He glances at me quickly, with a look of uncertainty on his face, and I exhale quietly with relief as he pulls over to the kerb. His hand stays on my knee as I try to open the passenger door.

'Don't get in strangers' cars if you're going to be a frigid bitch,' he says, and squeezes my knee until it hurts, before letting go and turning to look straight ahead, as if to say, this conversation is over.

I get out of the car, my heart hammering in my chest. The walk home, although only about two minutes, is frightening, as I am unsure whether he will come after me.

I feel a wave of sweet relief as I close the front door behind me and tell myself that I won't be getting in a stranger's car again.

I make a point of catching up with the ten o'clock news on TV when I get into my bedroom. Footage of the Libyan embassy siege plays out on the screen. Why did I dream of this?

Since the visitor has cropped up, my dreams seem to come true in some way or other. Do I become more psychic for some reason and that opens my senses to sense and feel the visitor? If that's the case, he must visit me all the time and I don't fully realise. Or he makes me more psychic when he visits.

Either way, no wonder I am so tired all the time.

5

Today is a wonderful day. It is Good Friday, or 'Great Friday' as we call it. I'm not religious in any way. For me, it's all about the chocolate and having some time off school. Mum and Dad have bought us some Easter eggs; I've spotted them in plastic bags on top of Mum's wardrobe. Although I love chocolate, I plan to sell mine to my sister as I am on a diet, in a last-ditch attempt to lose some weight for next weekend, for a party at Anna's. Alice probably hasn't got much money, so I may end up getting her to tidy my bedroom as a swap.

My new diet involves eating an apple for breakfast, no lunch and then a 'normal' dinner at home, but I only eat my favourite part of it. In the canteen at school, our group fill up our lunch trays with bread rolls and butter and any packaged foods that are easy to sell. We then sell our food to the boys, so it's double whammy as, a) we are getting slimmer, and b) we are making money. I also plan to get some extra help as there is an older girl at school who is selling laxatives that look like miniature chocolate bars. Most of us are on a diet. Well, the girls are. We all want to look like Cindy Crawford but, we all look more like Cyndi Lauper.

Mid-morning, Mum called me downstairs and Layla was on the phone for me. She invited me to come over to her house today. Dad drives me to Layla's house, which is about twenty minutes away. He is angry with me because he thinks I have been watering down his alcohol. I deny it, of course. At one point he calls me selfish, and I am so offended that I slam the car door hard when I get out and he drives off angrily. Always angry.

As I approach the house, I feel a strong sense of déjà vu. I feel like I have been here before, but in a dream. The houses are all joined together, tall and thin, and kind of old-fashioned looking, like the houses you see in *Eastenders*.

Layla answers the door and I must stifle a laugh. I had expected her mum to answer the door, but Layla stands there, looking tiny, like a shrunken adult, and it catches me off guard.

I go inside the narrow hallway which is very "busy", as my mum would say, and cluttered with pictures on the wall. As we walk our way through to the kitchen, which is down some steps, I can see it is the same in here too. It's kind of nice, with Laura Ashley wallpaper and a pine table on the left, with two chairs.

There are pictures on one entire wall and lots of candles and joss sticks dotted around the surfaces. There's a stone Buddha statue sitting on the window ledge and someone has put some red flowers over the Buddha's lap. A sensation of déjà vu yet again. I

216

remember dreaming of flowers in my lap, but it was a negative feeling for some reason.

Layla rummages in a kitchen cupboard for some crisps to take upstairs with us, and she makes us both a cold drink of milk in a glass with Cadbury's Drinking Chocolate powder mixed into it, which goes all bubbly and lumpy on top. We head upstairs with our drinks and crisp packets. Walking into Layla's room, the first thing I see is her huge bed, and then a huge Ghostbusters poster on her left wall. The bed is amazing, a four-poster with Laura Ashley drapes. The drapes look like they could hide the entire bed, like curtains. I think how scary that must be, shut away in the bed.

'Do you ever close the curtains?' I ask Layla.

'All the time,' she replies. She clearly doesn't have any night visitors to worry about, I think. I won't be telling her about mine, then.

We have a good time, munching on way too many crisps. Layla gets up at one point, telling me she has a surprise. She goes out of the bedroom, then a few minutes later she bursts back in, with a kind of running jump, and as she lands with her knees bent, she says, 'Ta-Da!'

I burst out laughing, as her movements remind me of a frog, and I see she has a packet of Silk Cut in her hands.

'Whoa!' I say, impressed, and we smoke two cigarettes, one straight after the other, until we feel dizzy. We sing Lionel Richie's 'Hello' out of her bedroom window. We have a look through Layla's mum's drinks cabinet and find some Eggnog. It is truly disgusting, but we manage to drink half of the bottle between us. I feel really drunk and I am so close to telling Layla about my dreams and, especially, about my visitor. I am just about to tell her, and my mum rings on the front door to pick me up.

In the car, Mum accuses me of smelling of cigarettes, but I blame it on Layla's mum, even though Layla's mum wasn't even there. Layla had told me that her mum was on a training course for the weekend, to learn something Indian sounding.

Before bed, I try to read a chapter of my new book, *Pet Sematary* by Stephen King, my favourite author. I am still a bit drunk, so I keep repeating the same pages over and over and eventually give up. I have started to collect all of Stephen King's books, and I like them so much that I can read them again and again. I like to fully immerse myself in the stories and pretend that I am there experiencing everything. But unlike some of my friends, I don't find the books scary.

My real life is much more frightening.

6

On Easter Sunday morning, Mum and Dad give us our Easter eggs. I get seven eggs from various family members and decide to sacrifice six of them and keep the huge Cadbury's Roses egg. I persuade Alice to take my assortment of six eggs and in return, she must tidy my room for six weeks, but to keep it from Mum and Dad. Alice seems happy with the deal.

After breakfast, Alex and her cousin Jayne knock for me, wearing their roller skates. I get mine on and we skate down to the park. I'm not the best on skates and on the way home I manage to crash into a flower display outside the greengrocers. I'm relieved when I get home and take the skates off.

I get back in time for the Top 40 on the radio, which I need to tape. I manage to tape some great songs. 'Lucky Star' by Madonna, 'PYT' by Michael Jackson, 'Somebody Else's Guy' by Jocelyn Brown and 'Just be Good to Me' by The SOS Band.

Mum calls out and interrupts me at one crucial point.

'Come down for dinner!' she says, but I can't possibly miss out on any good songs.

'I can't! I'm taping!' I yell back.

This tape will be excellent. I am learning most of the words, even the songs that aren't my favourites.

Another party tonight, this time at Anna's, the best location of all. Anna's parties are legendary amongst our group and not to be missed. This is for a few reasons. Anna's mum goes out, a lot. She stays over at her boyfriend's house for days at a time, which leaves the house free for parties. She is also a very relaxed mum and way less strict than my mum and dad. And Anna has her own den downstairs, which is where the parties are held. It's just the best fun. Most of us can't get into pubs yet and even if we could, we haven't really got much money, so house parties are the way to go.

I get myself ready, wearing my new tight white stretchy mini skirt with a white three-quarter length sleeved top with a strip of white tassels on the front, and I am so excited to show off my new haircut to Matt. I've kept it long in the back but it's shorter and layered in the front and on top. I love it. I put loads of layers of eye make-up on, which I copied from a model on the cover of *Cosmopolitan* magazine, but I leave my lips without lipstick for tonight, as I will be drinking lots and, hopefully, getting off with Matt.

I walk into Anna's kitchen and hear Shannon's 'Give me the Night' coming from the den; there are only a few of us here, but it will get busier soon. I unload my plastic bag which is filled with party goodies. I have managed to fill a huge plastic bottle that I found under the sink with a mix of my dad's alcohol from his drinks cabinet. He really should get a lock put on it. I poured mostly vodka, ouzo and gin into the plastic bottle. I chose these three drinks not for the taste, as they all taste horrible, but so that all the liquids are clear, and they would look like water if I got stopped with the bottle by my parents. I then topped up the alcohol bottles with water and placed them carefully back in the cabinet. Dad won't notice, I don't think. Even if he does, I don't really care as I will just deny it.

Along with the special "mix", I have bought a half-filled bottle of my favourite Martini Rosso which was also in the cabinet, and a packet of cigarettes.

I had struck lucky on the way to Anna's house. As I walked towards the little row of shops near the bridge, I saw two older boys, probably men, standing outside the sweet shop near the bridge, so I asked them politely if they could buy me some cigarettes if I gave them the money. They agreed to this and asked if they could come to the party with me, but I said no and pretended that our parents were also going to be there. As I walked away, I was very impressed with my on-the-spot lie, as they seemed to believe it. They followed me for a little bit, then must have drifted off because they weren't behind me when I arrived at the front door.

I sit with Anna on the sofa, and we muck around. Anna has a Kenwood HiFi that her mum's boyfriend has wired up to huge speakers. The sound is so good, a hundred times better than my stereo. She is very lucky because her mum will buy her pretty much whatever she wants. One of our favourite songs comes on, 'Red, Red Wine' by UB40. Everyone in the room knows the words, so we are all singing loudly, with John the twin, probably the loudest of us all, pretending to be Ali Campbell with a microphone.

'Red Red Wine, it's up to you, oo oo, all I can do I've done, memories won't go, memories won't go.'

Roly grabs a bottle of red wine and starts to drink it straight from the bottle, but John the twin makes him laugh and he spits a huge stream of wine on to the carpet. Anna runs over and hits Roly and he backs off, laughing. We call Alex 'Roly', as he looks like Roland Rat from TV-am.

Then I spot Matt. I am really pleased when he walks into the den. He's one of those boys who doesn't live near us, but he seems to know everyone. As he talks to a few people, I keep glancing over at him. He is wearing a light pink T-shirt and dark blue Farahs and looks very nice, but then he always looks good. He eventually comes over and sits with us on the sofa and tries to say something to me, but the music is too loud, so I can't hear him. The song playing is 'Ghostbusters' by Ray Parker Junior, and a few of the boys are doing a crazy dance or, more accurately, crazy movements in time to the music.

This song always makes me cringe. A group of us had gone to see *Ghostbusters* when it came out at the pictures. We always sat at the back, so that the only popcorn thrown would be by us and no one else. I had my feet up on the seat in front of me and when the lilac-coloured ghost popped up in the library, I jumped right out of my skin and managed to accidentally completely break the seat that my feet were on with the force of my shock. I'm still embarrassed about that, so the song reminds me of my Incredible Hulk moment, every single time.

We are all drinking a lot and I am sticking to my red Martini, straight from the bottle. The boys are all drinking beer, which I find disgusting; how can they like the taste? Helena comes over at one point, and she has had the same haircut as me, although her hair is blonde and mine is brown. I hope we don't all end up having the haircut, as we will look like carbon copies of each other. She is also wearing a skirt the same as mine but in bright blue, so she must have got it in C & A. Helena takes a photo of the three of us, which I can't stand. I try to get her to stop but she insists. Helena and her camera. I'm sure she will be a photographer when she's older.

I am getting more and more drunk and need some fresh air, so Matt and I go out of the patio doors into the back garden.

Once the cold fresh air hits me, I am badly sick. Matt is really kind, even though his shoes are splattered with my red-coloured vomit. I help him to wash the mess off with the garden hose that is attached to the wall, but I am still silly and drunk, so I go up his leg and wet his trousers. He manages to grab the hose from me and hoses up my legs and gets me in the face, on purpose. We end up grappling with the hose and drenching each other from head to toe.

We go back inside to the den, where everyone is laughing and going crazy at the sight of us, and a few of the boys and a girl pile outside the patio doors to have a water party of their own.

Along with Matt and Anna, a group of us all jump around in the middle of the room to the music, and then the tape starts playing 'Like a Virgin'. A Madonna song. Anna always sings 'Like a Zoe' when the song comes on, and I laugh along as it doesn't offend me and, to be fair, I am always talking about losing my virginity.

So, sure enough, we are all joining in singing along, leaping about like crazy drunk people. Legs and arms are flying about, bumping into each other, falling on the floor.

At one point I fall, and while I am on the floor, still soaking wet, I suddenly think Right, this is getting boring now. I stand up, swaying slightly, and say loudly

'Everyone!' It takes a minute or so for it to quieten down enough for me to announce:

'Right. After tonight, you will never ever be able to sing that song again!' and I grab Matt's hand and practically drag him out of the room, to the sound of cheers and whoops and, bizarrely, one scream. I half expect Helena to follow us with her bloody camera.

When we get into Anna's bedroom, things get very heated very quickly, and we manage to fall off the bed on to the bedroom floor. At one point, I get a quick flashback of Matt's evil face from my recent nighttime visit, but I shake it off.

So, I lose my virginity on Anna's rug. Afterwards, feeling more sober, I think, is that it? Matt practically struts out of the room with his chest puffed out, but I emerge from the room as if nothing had just happened. I feel nothing.

And I know. I just know. This is not my first time. I know that the nasty nighttime visitor was my first, but does that count?

7

The visitor came again last night. I wasn't just afraid when he came. I was also angry. I feel like I can't just be myself and have a normal boyfriend as he takes advantage of me because I can't move and it's just not normal. I wonder if Matt could somehow tell that I wasn't a virgin? He's not the sort of boy to spread gossip but it makes me sad that he might think that about me.

I'm frightened that if I don't tell anyone and he scares me too much, and I then have a huge heart attack in the night, no one will know why. I can't tell my mum and dad, it's too embarrassing, too personal. So, I decide to tell Layla. She will understand.

Early evening, I go downstairs and sit on the bottom stair to phone Layla. When she answers, I ask, 'What are you doing?'

'Nothing. I'm bored.'

'Can your mum drop you over?' I ask.

'She would probably love to,' she replies. 'I'm getting on her nerves apparently.'

I look forward to seeing her.

This is the first time that Layla will see my new hair. After school on Thursday, I went straight to the hairdressers in the village. The whole place smelt strongly of chemicals, probably perm lotion, but I really like the smell, even though it will give me a headache later.

Over on the left wall, a row of old ladies were sitting under huge hairdryers, looking like space aliens. As I sat and waited near the front entrance, I chose a picture of Sheila E from a magazine. Her hair is exactly how I want mine, curly and big but a bit shorter at the side. I was excited as the hairdresser cut my hair, but when she had finished my hair was all smooth and flicky, and I looked awful. I didn't say anything, but I think she could tell by my face. So, when I got home, I backcombed it for longer than usual, using Dad's black comb and lots of Mum's hairspray.

I can confide in Layla. She is not one of the usual group, but someone I now think of as special as she is mine only and lives in a different town. I think she is quite deep, in that she is open to talking about subjects that my other friends would struggle with. I don't think she would get on with the rest of the group, as she is different somehow.

I have dinner in my bedroom, Mum's chilli con carne. It's tasty, but I always must drink a couple of pints of water with it as its very spicy.

Layla turns up and we catch up on everything from Good Friday when I saw her last. She loves my hair, but her mum won't let her have any money for a haircut now because she lost their dog when she took him out to the woods. Why are parents so mean to us all the time? It wasn't Layla's fault; it was an accident.

We talk so much that we decide we need a drink and a treat, so I sneak downstairs. Mum and Dad are in the dining room with Uncle Pete, drinking wine and laughing. Mum spots me go past and calls me. I kind of reverse and tell her I am just getting some juice. They don't notice me as I sneak back past them with a Viennetta from the freezer and a carton of fresh orange. It's great when they have people over as they don't notice what I'm up to as much. Layla is pleased with my booty.

'Ah, shit, I forgot spoons. I can't sneak back down now.'

So, we hunt around for something we can use as a spoon to scoop up the ice cream with. Layla comes across a protractor in my pencil case, and we laugh as we scoop the ice cream into our mouths messily. We watch *Top of the Pops* on TV together and devour our ice cream. Nena is number one again, with a very catchy song '99 Red Balloons', and I notice that her hair is very similar to my new haircut. When we have finished our ice cream, I pop the protractor out of my bedroom window and Layla laughs and says I might squash an ant.

We sit together in my bedroom, Layla lying on my bed propped up on her elbow, smoking a cigarette and trying to blow smoke rings, without success, whilst I sit cross-legged on the floor, playing tapes on my new tape recorder.

'I need to tell you something.'

I tell Layla everything I know, from the weird experiences when I was seven to the visits that started again recently. I held back on telling her about the dreams that sometimes come true. That is a step too far and would make me sound deranged.

We talk through everything and, between us, we decide to name my visitor Jacob. Naming him makes me feel so much better. It is almost making him less scary, almost taking back some of the power. We try to "summon" him, with no luck.

While we are listening to music, I take the time to write down all the songs, as I have loads of tapes that I need to write labels for. I take out all the white lined inserts inside the plastic covers and grab some pens. We both love our music and listen to 'Little Red Corvette' by Prince three times in a row, as we both love the song.

While playing the tapes, the only buttons I pressed were "play" and "pause", pausing when it got to the end of the song and I hadn't managed to write down the name yet. I was just about to press play to hear the next song, and Stevie Wonder's 'Part-time Lover' began to play, without me pressing anything.

'Oh my God!' I started to giggle nervously.

'Quick!' Layla leapt off the bed and crouched next to me.

The song continued to play by itself. Peering closely at the tape recorder, the spools were turning round as they do when a tape is playing, but the play button was in line with all the other buttons and not pressed down. I briefly thought this could be a fault with the tape recorder but in the mood of the night, I didn't even mention it. I pressed play and the song just continued with no interruptions. We got over it quickly and proceeded to try to conjure up Jacob again, by teasing him and calling him a coward.

Nothing happened, so we chatted for a while about other things. We were fooling around and laughing, and a movement caught my eye, over to the left of the room.

'Whoa, look!' I pointed to the carpet on the other side of the room, whilst moving away by shuffling backwards on the floor. It looked like the carpet was raising slightly and kind of rippling, like there was air under it. I thought of the wave pool on our holiday to Spain last summer.

Layla's legs had been dangling over the edge of the bed, but they shot up off the floor as she panicked, and she curled her legs under her, kneeling up on the bed.

'Can you see it?' I say and she nods.

'The carpet is moving.'

We look at each other in shock and then descend into slightly manic nervous laughter. But the deep pile shaggy carpet is too thick to move. The movement is more like a shimmer, almost like the oasis that tricks thirsty people in the desert, just an illusion. My dad had explained this trick of the eye to me once, and it stuck with me. I moved further backwards to the bed, keeping my eyes on the shimmering carpet, and got up on the bed close to Layla.

'If you weren't here, I wouldn't be laughing,' I tell Layla, and she agrees.

'Yep, I'm okay with you here, but I'm going to try to forget this when I'm lying in bed tonight.'

I feel that when me and Layla are together and in this mood for scares, any strange activity ramps up by times two.

When Layla had gone, I got ready for bed, looking forward to watching TV before going to sleep. I like to lie flat on my tummy and lean on my arms as my TV is on a little bedside table at the end of my bed. My TV is my pride and joy. It's only small but modern with a white plastic cover. When I switch it on, I twiddle the knob to find the channel that *Blackadder* is on. Both the sound and the look of the black fuzzy screen between channels reminds me of Jacob's visits, so I turn the volume right down, and look slightly down, so that I can't directly see it, but I can still see when I reach my channel.

I was happily watching *Blackadder*, laughing at Baldrick, and I thought I dreamt of this last week. Then, suddenly, the sound coming out of the TV seems to be getting louder. I lean forward to turn down the volume knob, and my hand jumps back in fright. The knob is turning round to the right, slowly, on its own. I want to reach out and stop it turning, but it feels dirty somehow, and I don't know what I would feel if I touched it. I dart my finger out like I am prodding an angry bear and press the on switch to off. The dark screen somehow frightens me, so I grab my dressing gown and throw it over the TV.

This night has been too spooky. I decide that there's no way I'm sleeping in this room tonight. I quietly creep downstairs and sit on the sofa in the front room on my own. I make sure I sit on the sofa to the right of the room, which doesn't face towards the patio doors. I am frightened to see my reflection in the patio doors at night due to a nightmare I had when I was younger.

Mum comes in and asks if I'm okay. I tell her I'm not and ask if I can stay in their bedroom tonight, so she makes up a sleeping bag next to their bed for me. I feel a bit silly, as I'm fourteen now, but I feel like Jacob is somehow near now and I dread to think what other tricks he has up his sleeves.

Now I regret the joking about Jacob with Layla earlier. I think I have angered him. Everything is scaring me so much now. People are supposed to rest when they are asleep, and I am having a battle. I feel like I am doomed in some way. I think of what Mum always tells me when I get scared at night 'Everything will seem better in the morning.'

This is true, but day always leads to night.

1983

1982

1981
1980
1979
1978

PART SEVEN
7 YEARS OLD

1977 – 42 years ago
1

I can see some very tall stone steps curving round and round and they curl right up into the blue sky, but there's no building around them. I am standing on a beach and it's daytime, but I'm not with anyone else. The sun is in the sky but it looks like a drawing of the sun, it is yellow but not shining, and someone hasn't coloured it in properly.

Now I can see that there is a witch at the bottom of the very tall steps, but I know that she is not a mean witch at all, and I'm not scared of her. I think she is a good witch like Glinda from the Wizard of Oz, but she is dressed like a scary witch, as she is wearing a crooked pointy hat and a raggedy long black dress. She walks over to me and hands me my school satchel, and I know it's mine because it is bright red with a yellow star on it and my name is written on it in marker pen. That's very kind of her. I wonder where she found it. I open the satchel as it feels heavier than usual, and I pull out a story book and on the front cover there is a picture of the stone steps that we are standing in front of, and the nice witch's face is also on it.

I open the book and there is no writing on any of the pages. I keep on looking through the pages and it looks like the whole book is blank. I feel so sad that there are no words, but I don't want to act like a brat because the witch has been so kind. I am shy to tell her that it is empty inside, so I just say, "thank you". But I think the witch can tell by my face that the empty book had made me sad. I dig my hands deeper in to the satchel, and I find that there are lots of scraps of coloured paper, all shredded up. I don't know what they are, but they make me feel angry and sad at the same time.

I think this is supposed to be a scary dream as I can now see a ghost flying over to where I am standing with the witch, but he is friendly with a nice smile on his face. He looks quite silly, like a ghost from a cartoon. The ghost asks me to go with him and the witch to hide, because somebody nasty is coming. I go with them and we hide in a hole at the bottom of the stone steps, like a little cave, which just fits us all in.

We can see out, but nobody can see in. We then see a man, near a pile of rocks which are running from the sea to the beach, and he is looking around for us. He has a hammer in his hand kind of raised up, and he has a very black beard and quite big hair, but I can't see his face properly, his face is all blurry. He feels like a very bad man, so we are all as quiet as we can be. If he finds us, he will crush our heads in with the hammer. Even the ghost is scared and I don't even think he can be killed because ghosts are already dead.

I wake up and my bedroom is in darkness and it is still nighttime. The man with the hammer was very frightening, so I'm glad I have woken up before he got me, but the witch and the ghost were very nice. I must try to dream of something good now. I must think about nice things. Maybe the witch and the ghost, but not the hammer man.

I can feel that something bad is coming. It kind of feels like buzzy bees in my head. It is nighttime and very dark outside. I am standing in the back room, in front of the big, tall glass doors, a little way back from the glass. I can see my whole reflection, and I can see the brown leather sofa behind me, and the two glass lamps on the wall. But it doesn't feel like me. I am dressed in an old-fashioned fancy wedding dress, but it is black. I don't feel nice in this dress. I don't like black. I want it to be white if it's a wedding dress. There is a matching black veil over my whole head and face, and I can just see my face underneath and I look very sad. I don't like the feeling I have. It's a bad feeling, like when I see the daleks on *Doctor Who* or the wicked witch in the *Wizard of Oz*.

Then, behind me, reflected in the glass, I see Mummy and Daddy sitting next to each other on the sofa. They are smiling, but it's not a nice smile. I know it's not my real mummy and daddy. It can't be them: these two pretend people are mean. Or have my real mummy and daddy turned mean? I am getting more and more scared, and my tummy is hurting.

I look away from the mean mummy and daddy and look back at my reflection and I see that I am slowly lifting my arms up and pulling the veil back off my head. I look away from my reflection and look down at my own arms and they are still by my side, so my reflection can't be me.

My reflection's face has changed now, and I am pulling a very scary face; it's a mean smile, a very scary smile, and my eyes are big and open, and this is not me, I'm not mean. This is someone horrible pretending to me.

The buzzy bees in my head get louder. The boogie monster is coming. I am so scared, I start to scream.

I have woken up screaming but there's no sound coming out, the sound is just in my head. I want to run to Mummy and Daddy's room, but I can't move my body at all. It's happening again. Mummy! I can't even call out.

'It's okay,' Mummy would say. 'It's just a bad dream,' and, 'It's not real.' Maybe it *is* just another bad dream that is tricking me. But it doesn't feel like a dream because I can see my fluffy slippers on the floor where I left them, and I can see my Hollie Hobbie dolls, Amy and Carrie, lying on the chair in the corner. When I play with them, I like to pretend my whole bedroom is their whole house. My bed is their front room, so when I go to bed, they go to the chair which is their bed. Amy wears a green dress, and she has a happy face, and Carrie wears a red dress, but she has a sad face. Also, Benji, my fluffy toy dog, is in his bed, which is made up of a knitted blanket that my Grandma made me. I look over at Alice and see that she is fast asleep.

I look at the clock on the wall and the little hand is on the two and the big hand is on the one, which I think means five minutes past two. Everyone in the world must be asleep apart from me.

The bedroom feels wrong in my head and in my heart, but the only wrong thing that I can see in my bedroom is the rocking horse, which is rocking all on its own. Mummy! I really don't like this. My head starts to hurt, and the buzzy bees get louder. Behind my eyes it goes all fuzzy, like a fuzzy television. This is scarier than my dream. I must not think about Mummy and Daddy's mean smiles, but I can't help it.

Then I can feel the covers lifted off my feet and I know he is close. I close my eyes tight, and I feel the boogie monster starting to crawl up my bed. I feel cold water under my legs and then I know that I have wet the bed. I feel like a stupid, scared baby. *Keep your eyes shut, try to think of something to make him go away. I can't talk to him to ask him to go away because he has taken my voice away, so I will try to send my thoughts to him. Can monsters know what people are thinking?*

Please go away, I am only little, I am just seven years old. Maybe you think I'm older because I am tall

241

for my age. If I tell my mummy and daddy, they will phone the police.

The boogie monster doesn't stop what he is doing, even though I have wet the bed, so I go inside my brain and I find my happy place.

Storytime, with my favourite Jamie and his Magic Torch. Jamie's mummy tucks him in to bed and says, 'Sleep well, Jamie', but I change Jamie's mummy into my mummy. Then Wordsworth brings me my magic torch because I am now Jamie. I shine it on the floor, and it makes a big white circle on the carpet and, together, Wordsworth and I jump into the circle and slide into Cuckoo Land, landing on the trampoline. We jump and jump for a while and see how high we can go. Then we jump off and have a hug. Wordsworth has changed to Benji. Benji doesn't notice I have wet myself, so I am very happy about that. Wordsworth has such a funny voice, like a very old man, but Benji's voice is much nicer, as Benji is only seven, like me. Well, he is only one really, not seven, as I got him for my birthday when I was six, but I like to pretend he is seven like me.

Benji is so cute and gorgeous. He's a St. Bernard dog, huge and fluffy, and Mummy bought him in Jones' Brothers for me because I saw him sitting in a pile of teddies and I fell in love with him. Me and Benji go for a nice walk and the sun is shining in the sky and I can see a beautiful butterfly fluttering about near the flowers on the side of the shiny path we are walking on. The lady butterfly can speak, and she says, in a voice that sounds like Mummy, 'What a lovely day! Look at the sunshine!'

I can feel my arms being pushed down but I get that out of my head, as I am in Cuckoo Land now. Benji is very excited because he loves Cuckoo Land as much as me. It is such a lovely place, with no nighttime, ever!

Up ahead, on the winding, bumpy path, we see Officer Gotcha coming over the hill. When he reaches us, he asks if we have seen any ghosts and I tell him that ghosts aren't real. Me and Benji start to walk away and Benji then says 'Yes, Zoe, they are real. Open your eyes!'

'No, Benji!' I say, feeling angry and sad at the same time. 'You are trying to trick me. This is my dream, not yours!'

Benji runs away and I am left all alone.

'Come back, Benji!' I call out.

'Don't leave me alone!'

But Benji is nowhere to be seen and I think that he was not my Benji at all, but a mean one, trying to trick me to open my eyes. I start to feel cold, and Cuckoo Land starts to get darker.

I look up at the sun in the sky and a huge black cloud is passing over it, turning daytime into nighttime.

2

I can finally move, and I must get out of my bedroom as fast as I can. I jump out of bed and my head is thinking faster than my legs because I trip over and fall on to the floor. Alice wakes up from hearing my fall and she starts to cry. I quickly get up and run straight towards Mummy and Daddy's bedroom. As I run, I am trying to talk, and it comes out as screaming. I'm glad my voice is making sounds finally, but I'm hurting all over. My tummy hurts, my throat hurts and my chest hurts. I think my heart might be trying to jump out of my body.

When I reach Mummy's bed, she is already sitting upright and looking very afraid of my screaming. Poor Mummy, she was probably dreaming a nice dream. Mummy holds me close and speaks in a sleepy voice, 'What, Zoe, what's wrong?' I try to talk but I'm not making sense, my words are all jumbled up as I am crying so much, and my throat is stopping me talking normally. Mummy starts to calm me down and Daddy moves closer to Mummy and rubs her back to make her feel better. Mummy turns to Daddy and asks him to see to Alice, then she cuddles me close to her.

'Oh Zoe, you've had a wet night.'

I feel so shy about this. Alice is three years old, and she doesn't ever have wet nights. How can I be the big sister when I am more of a baby? Daddy gets up to go and see Alice, who is crying loudly now. As Mummy cuddles me, I can feel her heart beating as fast as mine.

'Come on,' Mummy says, and she takes me to the bathroom to help me to clean up.

As we walk past my bedroom on the way to the bathroom, I can still feel that nasty feeling coming from the room, kind of like the buzzing from the fridge when it is open, but scary. I look in, and Daddy is sitting on Alice's bed, rubbing her back to try to get her back to sleep. Mummy is being kind about being woken up, but I can tell she is very tired by her face and her messy hair. I don't think Alice or Mummy or Daddy can feel the buzzy feeling. I look up at Mummy's face and she doesn't look scared at all. Just sad.

In the bathroom, Mummy runs a small bath for me, but we only have cold water at nighttime, so I only have a quick wash with a flannel and soap. While I'm washing, I look up at the bathroom cabinet on the wall, which has a mirror on the front. I think of myself in the black wedding dress. It is too high for me to see into, so I don't have to see anything in it. I clean myself a bit quicker so I can get out of the bathroom.

When I am cleaned up and have my clean nightie on, I sit on the end of Mummy and Daddy's bed while my bed is made up. Mummy and Daddy ask what I dreamt of that made me so scared. My brain is telling me not to tell them, so I say that I dreamt of clowns. I am not even scared of clowns, but my friend Lucy is very scared of them, so I know they are frightening to some people. At my last birthday party, Lucy's mummy had to take her home when she saw the clown arrive at our house. I don't even think I'm scared of ghosts, but I'm frightened of the boogie monster. I can't tell them about him, but I don't even know why. The words just won't come.

Mummy makes me a comfy bed on the floor next to their bed and, as I snuggle down, I plan to stay awake if I can. Maybe even all night long.

I always have bad dreams, but they have got worse lately and some of them feel so real. Daddy tucks me in every night, always tucking me in tight so the hands can't crawl up my bed. I did tell Daddy about the scary hands, and he laughed and said I have watched too many scary programmes on the television, but he is always happy to tuck the covers over and under my feet very tightly. I am mostly not scared before I go to sleep and I think everything is going to be all right, but then sometimes the boogie monster comes. I get tricked by him every time.

I call him boogie monster because I don't know his name. I know he is some type of bad thing, from a bad place. He makes me feel very unhappy because I know he is mean. Mummy doesn't know about him, but she always tells me to be nice to people and not be mean to anyone, so I am kind. So, I don't understand why he is mean to me.

First, he kind of tells me he's coming but not by speaking, he tells me by getting inside my brain and making me feel dizzy, then he likes to start with my feet; I don't know why he likes my feet so much, my feet are yucky, but he likes to take the cover off them. Even when Daddy has tucked me in properly. How can he do that when Daddy has tucked me in so tight? He must be so strong.

He makes my body freeze so I can't walk, talk or move, I can only think. So, I find a happy place to go to which is my stories. I love my stories so, so much. If I make up a nice story, I kind of still know he's in my bed, but he is pushed into the back of my head, like when I am watching television but also playing with a toy at the same time. Then, if Mummy asks me about the programme I am watching, I can't tell her everything, only some things.

When he has gone, I do babyish things like scream and run in to Mummy and Daddy's room.

The other day, I heard Mummy telling Uncle Pete that I sleepwalk at night. I don't ever remember doing this.

I think Alice must be Mummy and Daddy's favourite daughter because she sleeps like a good girl all night and doesn't have wet nights.

Even though I really want to stay awake all night now, I'm finding it very difficult, as my eyes are so droopy that I can't fight it off any more.

3

In the morning, Mummy lets me push the buggy on the way to Alice's nursery. I try not to bump into bushes and when we see dog poo, Mummy takes over, making sure the wheels don't squidge through it. Alice hates the buggy, but she must sit in it today as Mummy is in a rush to get me to the doctors on time after we drop off Alice. We walk towards the scary bridge and Mummy chats all the way through because she knows I am scared. I just look straight up at her and she doesn't seem scared at all. I try not to think of monsters.

I can't wait to be a grown up, not scared of anything. But Mummy is afraid of spiders and loud bangs, so I will probably fear them too. It is quite cold this morning, so I have on my woolly hat. Mummy is cross because she thinks that I lost my matching scarf and mittens. I have lost my scarf, but I didn't really lose my mittens. This morning, I hid them away because they make me feel babyish. Mummy will never find them, as they are hidden inside a dolly's handbag in Alice's toybox. I have also hidden my red Hollie Hobbie doll, Carrie, in Alice's toybox, right at the bottom.

Carrie's sad face was making me feel angry. I don't know why she is sad as she is not a real person.

Once Alice has been dropped off at nursery, we walk to the doctor's in the village. It is warm in the doctor's waiting room, and it smells of Germolene. I love that smell. I asked Mummy the other day if I could make some Germolene perfume, but she said no. She showed me how to make rose perfume, by putting rose petals into a glass bottle of water, but I don't really like the smell. It smells of very old ladies in flowery gardens to me.

Mummy has brought me to the doctor's because she is worried about my bad dreams and wants to ask the doctor for help. Mummy sits down in a chair facing the ladies who answer the telephones and I go off to explore the play area. There is a pile of toys and books in the corner of the room, so I go for the books. I see a Paddington Bear book. I do like Paddington, but then I see another book that I am interested in more. The book has a witch on the cover creeping down some steps. It's called *The Great Ghost Rescue*. I feel like I have seen this book before, but I haven't got this at home and I haven't seen it at school, so where? I really want to read this book to see if I can learn how people can rescue ghosts, but I really don't think I have enough time, as the doctor will call us in soon. I want to keep this book and take it home. It is a bit old and ripped but I don't care.

I start to read the book and all I manage to find out is that the ghost is called Humphrey Horrible. Then, suddenly, Mummy comes over and takes my hand.

'Zoe, come on, it's our turn.'

I get a bit panicky as I have still got the book in my hand when we walk into the doctor's room, but I don't want to let it go.

There is a lady doctor sitting behind a desk and she does a smile which is not really a smile, she is just lifting her lips up.

'How can I help you?' the doctor says, when we sit in the chairs in front of her. She is a bit scary because she has big hair like the queen, and she doesn't feel friendly. She doesn't even look at us much. The man who was our doctor before was much nicer.

Mummy tells the doctor about my sleepwalking and bad dreams. I don't talk at all, I just nod or shake my head when the doctor asks me something. Mummy talks for ages and I stop listening as I am thinking about the book in my hand. Maybe if I keep holding it, they will think it is mine? And I can pretend that I forgot it was in my hand and we could bring it back to the doctor's for other children to read when I have read the book. Mummy has told me that stealing is wrong. But I think I'm just borrowing this book as I will bring it back.

When Mummy starts to stand up and thanks the doctor for her time and the doctor does her pretend smile, I am surprised that they have finished already. That was quick. Mummy leads me out of the doctor's room and through the waiting room, to the front door, and I clutch the book tightly. Mummy hasn't noticed. I feel sad though. Mummy is being kind, but I am sad that I can't have some medicine to make the boogie monster go away.

When we get outside, Mummy asks whether I understood what the doctor said.

'Yes, I've got to stop watching *Doctor Who*.'

Mummy smiles, and says 'Also, she said that you have a very vivid imagination. That means you can imagine things easily, so that causes your scary dreams.'

I feel sad and a bit angry. So, it is my brain's fault. How can I stop my imagination? Maybe I can pretend to turn my brain off at bedtime. I will try that when I go to bed tonight.

When we get near to school, Mummy sees her friend Jackie and stops to talk to her. As they talk, I put my secret book in to my school satchel. I can't wait to read it later. If the doctor can't help me with some medicine, maybe the book can help me to learn all about ghosts and how to help them go away.

When Mummy and Jackie have finished chatting, Mummy walks me in the school gates and takes me right up to my classroom as I'm shy to go in late. But all the other children are in assembly, so it's just me and Patricia who are sitting at our desks in the classroom. I kiss Mummy goodbye and she rushes off to go to her cleaning job.

Patricia isn't allowed to go into assembly because she doesn't do the same prayers as us. She's a bit different to the rest of the class as she wears a scarf over her long hair and different clothes to the rest of us girls. Patricia doesn't believe in the same god as us. I don't even believe in our God, but I never tell anyone that. Surely God wouldn't let a boogie monster scare and hurt me? Maybe I could find out about Patricia's god.

I am very sad about Father Christmas too. Jack in our class has a grown-up brother so he knows more than all of us, and he told us that Father Christmas is really our daddies delivering the presents and the Tooth Fairy is really our mummies leaving a penny under our pillows. So, there is no nice magic. Only bad. I wonder if my friends know about the bad magic. Does the boogie monster visit them?

It's dinnertime, and Alice and I sit at the table in the front room. Mummy has given us minced beef with peas mixed in, with mashed potatoes. I also have a cup of my favourite fresh orange juice that the milkman delivers in a milk bottle. Alice is sitting on a cushion to help her reach the table, and I see Alice's crayons and some paper scraps ripped up next to her. I wonder what they are, so I pick up a scrap and I burst into tears as I see that the rubbish was once my favourite paper dolls that Uncle Pete had got me for my birthday. My lovely paper dolls are ruined because stupid Alice has ripped them apart. I am so angry, I get up and grab the papers and scream at Alice.

'Stupid baby!'

Alice cries and Mummy comes in the room and gets really cross at me for shouting. But I can't stop crying and I start to hit my head with both my hands because I am so angry and upset. Mummy gets down on her knees and holds my arms down to try to get me to stop, but I can't.

When I have calmed down, I say sorry to Alice, but I don't think she understands, as she is only three years old. Mummy is being kind, and she says I should go up to my bedroom and have some time alone without Alice, so I go up into my bedroom and start to read my secret book. It turns out that Humphrey Horrible is nice and kind. The real boy in the story, Rick, is not scared of ghosts at all, even Humphrey's horrible brother, George. The book is all about rescuing ghosts and I can't find any ideas in the book on how to get rid of the boogie monster. But it's a fun book anyway, just not helpful or scary to me.

Mummy comes in and tells me it's time for my bath, so I hide my secret book under my pillow. While I'm having a bath before bed, Mummy is busy cleaning the sink.

'Mummy.'

'Zoe?'

'I really don't like our rocking horse any more.'

'Why not?'

'It's scary.'

'It's no scarier than it's ever been. Remember what the doctor said about your imagination?'

So, I have decided that I will not look at the rocking horse, especially at nighttime, ever again.

Mummy lets me stay up a little bit later, so that Alice can get sleepy before me. Also, she has a surprise for me. Mummy has made me some new paper dolls herself and coloured them in with felt-tip pens. I'm so happy that I make her a thank you card with glitter and rose petals glued on to the front.

As I sit down to play with my paper dolls, the boring news comes on. I see something on the news about a very bad man called the Yorkshire Ripper, who hits people with a hammer. Mummy wouldn't tell me why he is called the Yorkshire Ripper. I think he should be called the Yorkshire Hammer man. He has killed lots of ladies, but Mummy says he doesn't live near us, so not to worry. I am not worried, as I don't think he would pick me to kill even if he lived next door. I think he would get scared off by the boogie monster.

I'm allowed to stay up until nearly eight o'clock at night to watch *Some Mothers do 'Ave 'Em*. Me and Daddy always copy the funny man when he says 'Oooh, Betty!'.

It's bedtime, and I am lying in my bed; Daddy has tucked me in how I like it, the sheets pulled right up to my chin and tucked safely over my feet. He then kind of chops his hands to each side of my body and feet so I am properly tucked in, and he usually does the same for

Alice, but tonight she has fallen asleep already as it is late.

Alice just copies me, she doesn't have bad dreams, I don't think, but she wants to be the same as me. I wish I was the same as Alice with no bad dreams. Usually, as soon as Daddy goes out of the room, she kicks off the covers, so she's not scared like me. Everything is so much easier for Alice. It makes me feel jealous and then I feel sad that I feel jealous.

Downstairs, I can hear Mummy playing her records in the front room. I can hear one of Mummy's favourite songs playing, and she is singing along, to The Eagles Hotel California song.

'On a dark desert highway, cool wind in my hair, warm smell of colitas, rising up through the air'.

I wonder what colitas is. I think it's maybe some type of bacon because that smells so lovely in the summer.

I like summer bedtimes because they are not so scary. I wish there were no night times as I don't like them any more. Once I am all tucked in, Daddy then closes the curtains and leaves the door a bit open and he says goodnight.

Our curtains are dark blue, with spaceships and stars and aliens all over them. When it is still a bit light outside, and the curtains are closed, I can see the sunshine through the white stars. I like these curtains; I like to dream that I am in space flying about. Nothing can scare you in space because you can zoom away in your spaceship quickly. It's summertime so we can go to bed when it is still light and not dark outside.

Mummy comes in and kisses me nunnight. When I start to feel sleepy, I try to turn my imagination off, but it's very hard. I try to think of Mummy's song again, but I change the dark desert highway to a sunny desert highway. I am driving along in a pink Barbie car and Benji is beside me. No one can catch us in this fast car, not even the boogie monster.

I know the boogie monster is not a real person, but when I feel his hands, I know there are monsters.

2020 - Present day
4

In and out of consciousness for eternity, am I in heaven?
It's a lonely place, not what I thought it would be.
Where's everyone else? I thought my ancestors and
loved ones would be here. Anna? Luke? Grandma?
Maybe I am in purgatory.

Beeping sounds. It's hardly harp music. Where am
I? More to the point, *who* am I?

The smell of sharp disinfectant. Why do I like that
smell? I have a flashback to when I was young, walking
into Grandad's garage, finding his big shiny tin of
Swarfega, opening the lid and smelling the green gloop.
How I loved that smell, like petrol. I wonder now
whether the chemicals got me a bit high and that could
explain my lifelong love of chemical smells.

Pain overtaking me, pain so large that it diminishes
me to nothing. Bright lights, too bright! I don't know
why I am here in this white space.

Snippets of conversations, talking about someone
who was involved in a car crash. A woman. Who?

Intense itching and burning on my body. I am all
alone.

I dream of my babies. Where are they? Who's looking after them? This is what heartache feels like.

The woman in the car crash was me. What must I look like?

I realise that my darling children are grown up now, but where are they? I want to be with them. Wet on my face. I must be crying.

I'm so cold. Everything is white. Snow? I think I am in Antarctica in a snowstorm. My teeth are chattering and I'm lying down in the snow. Get up! I'm trying but I can't move.

I'm dying, the pain! Help me! Make the pain go away! The pain is rising, and I am shouting.

My eyes open and I squint at the blinding light and then see movement to my left. The nurse twists the blind pulley system cord to eliminate the dazzling light blazing through the huge windows. With the glare removed, the stark hospital room comes into focus.

'Let's get you some pain relief,' the nurse says, checking my vital signs on the myriad of colourful graphs on the incessantly bleeping monitor. I can't thank her, as my only means of communication is to blink. I like to think that the nurse understands the meaning of my pathetic blink. After all, I have been here for what seems like an eternity and, along with that thought pattern, the Simply Red song 'If you don't know me by now' pops into my head.

After administering the pain relief, the nurse leaves the room and back into the abyss I go.

5

With no clear memory of my first six weeks of hospitalisation, I only recall a range of sensations. I have been at this hospital for nearly four months now and the doctors and nurses have been angelic, patiently doing their best to fix me. My injuries were extensive.

The cause of the crash had been determined as the result of me going into cardiac arrest and veering off my lane. The impact of clipping another vehicle and crashing head-on into the central reservation completely crushed my dashboard. The car then flipped, and the emergency services found me lying in the road. I was found to have a serious head injury, with a hole in my skull leaving my brain exposed. The paramedics had to put me into an induced coma at the side of the road to try to stem a potentially fatal bleed to the brain.

In addition, I had suffered internal bleeding, a broken pelvis and a whole host of nasty lacerations.

Despite the catalogue of physical devastation, I have not seen, heard, felt or even sensed the visitor as far as I am aware for my entire hospital stay. Amazingly, there have been no dreams, no eerie otherworldly energy, no visits from him and, bizarrely, no traumatic dreams of the actual crash.

After all these years of having cryptic dreams, of being chased and hunted, of fear and confusion, and now nothing. And the peace is wonderful.

I have been told the gory details, but I choose not to think about them. My mind is a blank. By some type of miracle, both the driver and passenger of the car that I swerved in to escaped unscathed, and I took the full brunt of the accident. My driving days are behind me and I am at peace with this.

Darcy and Billy come to visit me a couple of times a week, sometimes together, sometimes alone. They have been coming to see me since the accident, but it's only recently that I have regained full consciousness. I have no memory of my 50th birthday. I've been told there was cake, balloons and family members singing *Happy Birthday* round my bed. The children tell me that I smiled briefly while they were singing.

Darcy has been sneaking sushi in for me. I say sneaking, I'm sure the nurses would be fine with it, but we like to be all cloak-and-dagger about it for a laugh.

Adam has apparently visited me a few times, but I have no memory of that either.

6

I can now sit up comfortably. Layla comes to see me, laden with the traditional grapes, which she demolishes, Evian water bottles and my iPad, along with an internet booster stick to improve the unreliable Wi-Fi. I begin by watching lots of documentaries and films on Netflix, catching up with all the new releases that I have missed. And then, after a few false starts, I begin to fill my waking hours and relieve my crushing boredom by finishing my story.

Writing also helps me to manage the pain. It's hard to get started as the pain is uppermost in my mind, but once I start to write and it starts to flow, my pain becomes secondary and, as time goes on, it lessens more and more.

I have researched the incubus demon and feel that this was the cause of my lifelong night visitor. Incubus is derived from the Latin "incubate", which means to lie upon, and dates to 2400 BC. Apparently, repeated sexual activity with an incubus could result in the deterioration of health, one's mental state and even lead to death.

And why the pattern of visits every seven years? All I can seem to find online that is even remotely connected, albeit tenuously, is that the number seven in China determines the stages of a female's life. A girl gets her milk teeth at seven months, loses them at seven years, reaches puberty at fourteen years (2 x 7) and reaches menopause at forty-nine (7 x 7). And those that believe in angels state that the number seven is related to inner wisdom, mysticism and inner strength. Apparently, if you notice the number seven, you should have more faith in your guardian angels but also your own abilities. How any of this could have helped me, I don't know.

My theory is like the Chinese connection with the number seven, in that I see the stages of womanhood as age seven, a child, age fourteen, puberty, age twenty-one, adulthood, age twenty-eight, motherhood, age thirty-five, working life, age forty-two, grown-up children flying the nest and age forty-nine, menopause.

I have no doubt that my demon was intent in causing my death by taking the wheel. As to why, I can only surmise that he didn't like the interference by the clairvoyant chanting the spell, as he had been with me for so long.

I do wonder why he picked me, but I don't dwell too much as I don't want him to take up any more of my time. For weeks I have been typing feverishly, straining my eyes, but the writing has truly been a purge, expelling the demon to move on. Battered and bruised, but free.

Layla tells me all about the Coronavirus sweeping the globe. I had heard snippets in my times of consciousness, but I hadn't quite realised the seriousness or wide reach of the pandemic. She explained that the country is currently in lockdown, and that we will all have to socially distance for an indefinite amount of time because new strains of the virus are emerging almost weekly. It all sounds very ominous, and I can't quite get my head around it all. I think of the films I have watched over the years related to pandemics and decide to gen up and watch them again to prepare myself for when I can go home. My vivid imagination hasn't left me, so I have visions of martial law.

On another visit, I asked Layla, 'Do you remember—'

I didn't finish my sentence, as Layla interrupted.

'Yes. I know what you're going to ask… that day before you turned off?' Layla said.

I nodded.

'I got an overwhelming urge to stop you going that way. I can't explain it, although I've thought about it constantly since. Just before the turning, I started to point towards it, and I started to feel panicky, and I just didn't want you to go that way.'

'Ah, okay. Honestly, I think it was fate. I really believe I would have crashed even if I had followed you and gone home via the country roads.'

'But the motorway, Zoe,' said Layla, tearfully.

'I know, but this was meant to happen for some reason. And he's gone.'

'Really?' Layla reached out her hand and covered mine.

'Yes,' I smiled.

7

I am recovering well from my injuries and today is a real milestone. It is physical therapy day, and I am feeling proud that I have managed to make it to the coffee machine in the corridor, with assistance but without too much pain.

My rehabilitation plan is on track with all the goals ticked so far.

I beam at my physiotherapist, Darmika, and she beams back with real warmth. As I look at her face, something clicks together in my mind, like the last piece of a puzzle. I think back to the three angels dream from my early forties.

The third angel, a tiny Indian lady wearing glasses, is my Darmika, a specialist in trauma rehabilitation, and she truly is an angel in my eyes. The patience, warmth and good cheer that Darmika displays every single time she is helping me is truly priceless and she is helping me move on to the next phase of my life.

We head slowly back to my room and when I am alone, I think of the angels dream again. I walked under the scary bridge in the dream, along with many other dreams over the years, and I think the bridge must represent my nighttime experiences. The graffiti on the walls of the bridge was the date of my accident, 11th December 2019, which I have no doubt was supposed to be the date that I died.

My first angel stepped out, in my dream and into my life, and is Dan, my hypnotherapist, who has enriched my life for the better. Did he heal the lines by my mouth? Don't be silly, Zoe. No angel on earth could do that if Creme de la Mer can't. I personally feel that he prevented the lines from getting deeper by giving me back my mojo and stopping me smoking and binge eating.

Although Dan couldn't remove the visitor from my psyche, I believe that it wasn't meant to happen at that time.

My second angel, who helped me in my dream and in my life, is Dana; she managed to remove the visitor from his attachment to me, even though he came back for one final battle.

So, Dan, Dana and Darmika are my three angels.

It is incredible to think that our lives are mapped out for us, and presumably we are all able to see our path if we concentrate on the messages and symbols in our dreams. Maybe we are not meant to know, maybe it is better to live in happy ignorance.

I will encourage my loved ones to listen to their dreams. But for all my efforts to decipher meanings from my dreams, I couldn't have prevented my accident. It was meant to be, and it played out as it was always going to.

I glance around the room, my eyes landing on my get well soon cards, and I focus on Layla's card, sitting on the side table next to my bed. Not your classic get well soon card from Layla, no surprise there, but a plain black card with an apt quote from Socrates:

The secret of change is to focus all your energy, not on fighting the old, but on building the new.

I am fifty years of age now. Battered, bruised but mentally whole and at peace with myself. I feel that now is the second chapter of my life, it is now my time.

But, reader, please know…

There are monsters.